PHOEBE'S LOCKET

By Wanda McMahan

Order this book online at www.trafford.com
or email orders@trafford.com

Most Trafford titles are also available at major online book retailers.

Printed in the United States of America.

ISBN: 978-1-4269-6301-8 (sc)
ISBN: 978-1-4269-6302-5 (e)

Trafford rev. 06/07/2011

www.trafford.com

North America & International
toll-free: 1 888 232 4444 (USA & Canada)
phone: 250 383 6864 ♦ fax: 812 355 4082

Chapter One

Disturbing News

"Someone's moving into Gardiner Hall," Phoebe said.

Mam looked up from the bubbling jam pot, face all pink, short hair plastered against her head in damp ringlets.

Phoebe stared at the misty spectacle of steam rolling up and around the stove with Mam's head floating in the midst of it like a genie without a body.

"There are mowing machines in the garden, and a man is pruning the lilac bushes. And someone," Phoebe went on, "is swinging a scythe." She reached for a fat strawberry, suddenly uneasy that she had given away her secret! What would she say if Mam asked her how...

"How do you know all that?" Mam stirred the jam, looking at her with a raised eyebrow. "Have you been climbing that tree again, young miss?"

Phoebe shook her head, touching her left arm and wincing at the painful memory.

The oak tree grew close to the stone wall. It had been a bit of a do to get into the lower branches, pulling herself higher and higher until she could see the grand stretch of garden on the other side. A broken arm was too dear a price to pay, it turned out, because she saw only tangles of vines along the wall, tall scraggly bushes with crooked unpruned arms reaching out in all directions, and a winding intrigue of weed-covered paths. Far away the manor house squatted in a mass of giant sycamores, like a crouching monster, its dark windows staring at her menacingly.

Some kind of small animal, perhaps a rabbit, had jumped from under nearby vines, and Phoebe gasped in fright before tumbling downward.

Mam came running, picked her up, and together they stared at the left arm, flopped over so queerly at the wrist. Phoebe began wailing vigorously, and Mam, her face white and chin quivering, kept shouting for Old Daniel, until he appeared, looking a bit put out with having to leave his pruning.

"Oh, my! Lass, you've fixed that one right proper," he murmured, peering at the crooked wrist, shaking his head mournfully. It seemed a strange thing to say, because to Phoebe, something felt very <u>unfixed</u>!

Phoebe remembered the rough ride to surgery in Old Daniel's gardening lorry, his mower and tools making such a clatter that people along the way looked up, astonished at the clamor. And she remembered the long six weeks in the cast. She would <u>never</u>, she promised, climb the tree again, and the memory of pain and a churning stomach made it a promise easily kept.

Any curiosity she felt about the adjoining manor and grounds, and she <u>did</u> feel some, was satisfied in another way; that loose stone in the garden wall, under the honeysuckle, slipped out with just a wee pull.

Twice she watched the land agent, Ambrose Stinchcomb, walk the grounds with people who stepped along the weedy paths gingerly, the ladies lifting skirts distastefully, and sitting for just a moment in the gazebo.

"Just looky-loos," Myrtle Stinchcomb confided to Mam later at tea, "not really interested in buying. Just," she lowered her voice to a raspy whisper, "<u>curious</u> about the manor and the goings-on over there!"

The last bit of cucumber sandwich disappeared between her lips, and a napkin was pressed daintily to the corners of her mouth. She accepted another at once, and Phoebe watched fascinated as the tea goodies, piled high on the tray, dwindled to a solitary scone. Mam didn't seem to notice, but kept pouring tea, listening, and smiling politely.

The Stinchcombs were the first friends Mam and Phoebe made when they moved from East Bristol to Chestershire. Mr. Stinchcomb let the cottage to Mam with the understanding that since it was part of Gardiner Hall property she could not expect to stay when the manor sold.

The thatched cottage had been used by the manor seamstress who was married to one of the groomsmen. It would, of course, be needed again by a new owner who would set to sprucing up the grounds and hiring household staff. Gavin Gardiner, the present owner, because of family troubles, had lost all desire to live at Gardiner Hall, and indeed, had left no orders to his previous manager to even keep up the place while awaiting sale.

Phoebe and Mam settled comfortably in the cozy stone cottage outside the wall, with Old Daniel, the Scot, hired to keep the vegetable garden free of weeds, and the small orchard trim and tidy.

They had been relieved when the old fellow knocked on the door soon after they moved in, asking if any help was needed about the place. Mam had worried about the mowing and pruning chores. She had her heart set on a nice garden, but doubted she could handle all the work even with Phoebe's help. So Old Daniel was welcomed gladly, becoming an important part of their lives.

Each morning Phoebe listened for the sound of his lorry rattling down the lane. Old Daniel almost always had a peppermint or a sweet from his missus' oven in his pocket. When Phoebe asked him about a sled for winter fun, he smiled broadly and nodded, "Aye, lass, I'll put ye in my scoop and give ye a merry ride down the lane!"

Just now as Phoebe had played under the oak, noises came across the wall: voices, a snip-snipping, the clickety-clickety rattle of something with moving parts, and the swish-swishing of a cutting blade.

Reaching through the honeysuckle she pulled the stone out of the wall and peeked through-holding her breath-even though surely no one could hear the slight scraping as the peep place opened. By moving her head back and forth from one side of the hole to the other, she could see the two mowing machines pushed by workmen she didn't recognize. But greengrocer Wakefield's son, Simon, was pruning bushes. And a village handyman, Thad Meriwether, wielded a scythe.

What does it mean, Phoebe wondered. Who has bought Gardiner Hall? Will they want our cottage for service people? Where will we go, Mam and me? There was nothing else to let when we came. Has Mr. Stinchcomb told Mam we must leave soon?

Phoebe pushed the stone back into place and made for the cottage with questions buzzing in her head like the bees around the hollyhocks. She could tell now by the frown puckering between Mam's brows that she knew nothing about what was happening.

Phoebe watched as the jam pot was carried to the table where the clean, hot jars waited to be filled. Mam ladled the jam into them carefully, wiped the rims, and set the pot under the pump.

"I'll ring up Ambrose Stinchcomb and see if Gardiner Hall is sold or just being tidied," she said. But at that very moment a familiar voice trilled cheerily from the front stoop.

"La la la 1a! Too busy for company? Do I smell something delicious?" It was Myrtle Stinchcomb bustling in from the parlor, patting her face with a flowery handkerchief, and waving it back and forth to stir a breeze.

She spied the jars of cooling jam. "Yes, I do! What beauties!" She clucked approvingly. "Won't that taste marvelous on biscuits!"

Phoebe could not keep her eyes from rolling heavenward in silent protest of Mrs. Stinchcomb's teatime appetite. But Mam pulled out a chair for their chattering guest, who sank down heavily, reaching over to pat Phoebe affectionately on the head.

"Has Ambrose called about Gardiner Hall?" She looked from Mam to Phoebe expectantly. "No? Well," she settled comfortably and rushed on.

"They'll be here in a fortnight. Going to get the grounds ready. The manager, Adam Mathers, is to see to staff, and open the manor. There will be <u>so</u> much to do, you know. All the furniture covered with dust shrouds. Rooms and rooms to be cleaned. Drapes, ovens, and the library! You can't imagine," she lowered her voice confidentially, "how many books are on those shelves! Floor to ceiling, mind you! They just closed it up and <u>left</u>, you know. Went to- I don't know where- to see doctors about the son and grandson. Well, now, <u>that</u> was a sad thing. He married against their wishes, you know. <u>Out of his class</u>! Those things," she wagged her head sagely, "rarely work out."

Phoebe wondered when the woman would tell them what was going to happen to <u>them</u>! She could see Mam was anxious, too. She kept looking at Mrs. Stinchcomb, and was sort of wringing her hands.

"Who bought it?" Mam asked softly.

Myrtle Stinchcomb stared at her blankly.

"Gardiner Hall," Mam said. "You were saying someone bought Gardiner Hall and would be here in a fortnight."

Mrs. Stinchcomb looked shocked. "No. Not at all! No. Gardiner Hall didn't sell. Adam Mathers called Ambrose to take it off the market. The family is coming back! Every last one of them from- oh, I don't know where- and <u>oh..here now..oh my</u>!"

Phoebe and Myrtle Stinchcomb stared as Mam stood up, groped to steady herself against the table, and then slumped to the floor in a dead faint.

Chapter Two

The Cottage

"It's the heat! This kitchen- too small for cooking jam on such a warm day! No air in here at all!" Mrs. Stinchcomb had Phoebe running back and forth wetting the flowery handkerchief under the pump and wiping Mam's pale face.

Mam's eyes fluttered open. She looked up at Phoebe and Mrs. Stinchcomb staring down at her wide-eyed. Myrtle Stinchcomb continued patting with the wet hanky while speaking soothingly.

"There now. You'll be fine. No, not yet," she gently pushed Mam back when she struggled to sit up. "Rest a bit more, Millie. Then we'll sit up a spell before you stand. Phoebe, one more time under the pump." She handed the kerchief to Phoebe who was away and back again so fast with the dripping cloth that Mrs. Stinchcomb tittered nervously.

"My sakes, child, you'll be stretched out here beside your mam if you don't slow down!"

Phoebe, on her knees, smoothed Mam's hair with one hand and patted her shoulder with the other. She felt easier when Mam smiled, reaching up her own hand to touch Phoebe's cheek.

There is something familiar about this, Phoebe was thinking. She remembered a time long ago. A banging on a door..Mam opening the door..someone in the shadows shouting in loud excitement. And Mam lying on the floor with people splashing water on her face.

Do I really remember, Phoebe wondered, or has Mam told me about Dada's accident so many times that I <u>think</u> I remember? The Dada she had never really known- for it all happened more than seven years ago when she was just over two years old. Mam had told her about how her gentle-hearted Dada, a fine teacher, was knocked to the street by a coach whose driver hadn't even stopped to find out if he were dead or alive. Mam had gone to the hospital daily for a long line, but it was finally over. Mam had found work in a pastry shop, and Phoebe did remember the times they had tea parties with a sweet or sugar dolly from the shop.

It was on an evening last February that Mam had taken Dada's fine leather bag from the shelf. Phoebe watched as she pulled a smaller pouch from it, loosened the drawstring and turned out a horde of gold sovereigns that seemed to cover the table top. Phoebe had gasped as the coins whirled around, some on their edges, turning, twirling, until they all clattered to a glittering rest.

"I've quit at the shop, Phoebe. I'm going to take Dada's savings to the market for exchange, and all of it with what I've saved these seven years will keep us until I work again. We're going away. To a new place," she said.

"<u>Where</u>? <u>Going where</u>?" Phoebe stared across the shining coins at Mam's determined face. Phoebe knew no other place. There were no grandparents, aunts, uncles. <u>No one</u>! No other place in the world except these two cramped rooms over the cobbler on Briar Street in East Bristol. No other people except the cobbler and his wife who tended Phoebe while Mam was away at the pastry shop.

Mam told her they were going to a nice village- Chestershire- in the Cotswolds. They would rent a cottage, have a garden, Phoebe could play outside in the sunshine, and wouldn't that be just wonderful? Phoebe supposed so.

After packing, sweeping the flat clean, leaving a message with the cobbler of their destination, they took a coach to Burnstall Fell. A farmer carried their boxes, valises, and the two passengers on to Chestershire. He stopped right at the land agent's office next to the apothecary and agreed to wait while Mam inquired.

Taking Phoebe by the hand, Mam entered Ambrose Stinchcomb's business showing no sign of uncertainty or misgivings. It seemed to Phoebe that her mam acted for all the world as the Queen, Herself, as she stated her business to the man behind the desk.

Phoebe liked Ambrose Stinchcomb right off. He was a short, chubby man with a ruddy, cheery face, and twinkling blue eyes behind gold-rimmed spectacles. When he talked, he removed his spectacles and swung them in vigorous circles by an ear piece. The thought of how fast and in what direction they would fly if he let go, fascinated Phoebe.

There were no vacant dwellings in Chestershire, he said regretfully, but there was this cottage on Gardiner Hall land, part of the manor property for sale, and if she liked it, he could ring up the old gentleman's manager, and inquire if it could be rented until something else became available.

"Or," he added apologetically, "until the manor sold and the cottage along with it. In that case.." his voice dwindled away, but the meaning was clear.

Mam didn't hesitate, but said she would take it unseen and be glad to make do, and to please ring.

It was all settled so quickly. The call made, Mam with Phoebe back in the farmer's lorry, and using the directions given by Ambrose Stinchcomb, they were on their way. Down a winding tree-lined road, past cottages, a stone church, garden spots that must be lovely in spring, and finally they drove along the high stone wall surrounding Gardiner Hall. The lorry stopped in front of the cottage, and the three of them sat looking at the neat sturdy house.

"You and the young one will like this fine, Missus," the farmer said. "I'll carry your things inside and be on my way, or the woman will have the constable called out," he joked.

Mam paid him and thanked him gratefully. She and Phoebe hurried down from the lorry and up the path to the front door. Mam used the key Mr. Stinchcomb had given her, and the farmer set their belongings inside. He tipped his hat and was gone, leaving them alone in their new home.

They walked through silently, awed by the sunny parlor with plump pillows on a couch which showed only a hint of a sag, the kitchen with a pump over a stone trough, a large shelf-lined pantry, and an open hearth.

"Nice," Phoebe was moved to say, remembering water carried from the yard pump on Briar Street.

"Yes, it's nice," Mam agreed, and Phoebe could tell she was pleased.

The bedroom had a bed with a feather-ticking mattress, and when Mam opened the big cupboard on one end of the room and they discovered a small bed that pulled down, Phoebe clapped her hands in delight.

When Mam unpinned her hat and put it on the dresser, all at once Phoebe felt a burst of joy she couldn't put into words. This darling cottage was home! No matter the possibility of having to move later... for now, they were home!

They walked through the rooms again, looking out windows and finally, opening the kitchen door to the outside. There was the big oak. That would be the very place Phoebe could play.

"What's over the wall, Mam?" Phoebe asked curiously.

"Gardiner Hall grounds. No one lives there now," she said, sounding a bit sad. "But perhaps, someday a family will live there again." Phoebe felt sad, herself, considering when that happened she and Mam would lose this little home she already loved.

Within the week they met Myrtle Stinchcomb while shopping at the greengrocers. She accepted an invitation to tea, and became a regular visitor. Myrtle delighted on passing on gossip tidbits, being especially eloquent about the family who owned Gardiner Hall. Phoebe couldn't help but listen enthralled to the tale about the young man who left the manor to attend Cambridge. He up and married a girl he met in a book shop. She was a clerk!

Imagine! A fine young man heir to wealth and property. The father, Gavin Gardiner, disowned the lad. Forbade his ever returning home. The poor mother, whispered the servants around, saw him one time afterwards, and was severely reprimanded by the master. She died, poor lady, broken-hearted by the estrangement.

And then, some years back, wonder of wonders, the father received word from a hospital in Bristol that the son was there, a victim of amnesia, but identified positively by a Cambridge professor. Gavin Gardiner brought his son home, saying not one word about the existence, if any, of a wife. And even now, some six or seven years later, the poor man still doesn't remember who he is, or anything about his life before his illness. And if <u>that</u> wasn't enough tragedy, his widowed sister was back home with a young son who was blind! And <u>he</u>, the servants vowed, was a nine-year-old hellion!

Gavin Gardiner had decided to sell the estate and devote his life to finding a cure for his daughter's boy and his own son. The whole thing sounded so romantically mysterious to Phoebe.

But now she forced her thoughts back and helped Myrtle Stinchcomb get Mam up from the floor to a chair. Mam was insisting she felt fine, and Mrs. Stinchcomb finally left, following a stern admonition to Mam about resting, and urging Phoebe to see to her mam.

Later that day Mam sent Phoebe to the bedroom chest for the black valise. Phoebe felt a stir of anticipation as Mam used a little key on the lock. She took out a small box, setting it on the table in front of Phoebe.

Slowly Mam opened the box. Phoebe looked at the most beautiful thing she had ever seen: a burnished round gold locket, delicately embossed with gold leaves and entwined roses on a thin filagree chain. Phoebe had to catch her breath at the utter beauty of the thing.

"This is your locket, Phoebe." Mam pressed a tiny spring and the lid sprang open, showing a portrait of a solemn, rosy-cheeked baby.

"And this," said Mam, smiling tenderly, "is a portrait of your dear Dada."

Chapter Three

Robbie

Throughout the following days, sounds echoed across the garden wall. Several times Phoebe pulled out the loose stone to see what was going on. She gawked in amazement at the lawn, now neatly trimmed, and the flower beds, cleared of scraggly growth, prettily bordering swept paths. Vines had been cut back from the gazebo, and the structure, itself, radiated the beauty of two coats of fresh white paint. In her direct line of vision sat a stone bench, nestled in a half-circle of lilac bushes. Spring was nearing with its exciting promise of the leafing, budding, blooming miracle.

On her own side of the wall, Old Daniel was working his own magic; the garden plot was marked off, the soil warming up for a good turn-over before planting, the fruit trees looking free of blight.

"Will we have cherries and peaches?" she asked.

"Aye. That is," he eyed her carefully, "if the birds and other thieves leave 'em be, lass."

"Birds don't know any better," she said.

"Aye. But those other robbers I speak of, lass-they're the two-legged kind and have a bigger stomach. And sometimes," he went on, "some of 'em aren't very old." His eyes crinkled with mischief.

Phoebe watched him amble off. She liked Old Daniel. He didn't ever scold or make her feel like he was just watching to see what she would do wrong. He treated her with the genuine good humor a person uses with a friend.

One morning she heard new sounds from over on the other side of the wall. Voices. Different from the workmen talking back and forth. She listened at the wall closely. One voice sounded young. Another, older, slower. The voices were close, very close.

The family must have returned to Gardiner Hall, Phoebe realized. She thought about taking the stone out and getting a look at whomever it was. She inched it out slowly, for with no other sound to cover the slight, rough scraping, surely it could be heard.

"What was that, Grandfather? I heard something like one stone against another, a rubbing."

Two people were sitting on the stone bench facing the wall--a young boy about her own age, and a frail white-haired old gentleman wearing a shawl around his shoulders. The boy was looking straight toward the peep hole.

Phoebe sucked in her breath. How could he hear such a small sound? She stood very still, not daring to make any movement that would catch his eye.

"I heard nothing, Robbie. It's those good ears of yours again, my boy; good enough as I tell your mother to hear an earthworm burrowing in the ground."

"Just listen to the birds singing, Robbie! It's good to be back at Gardiner Hall. It looks so beautiful. The lawn newly trimmed, flowers getting ready to bloom. You'll be smelling the roses and lilacs, my boy. Oh, I'm glad to be home again and watch this early spring beauty!"

The boy was still looking toward the peep place where Phoebe's eye was watching. But he wasn't really looking, she realized. This Robbie was the wild blind boy Mrs. Stinchcomb told them about. Phoebe locked at him critically. So..he's not really looking, she concluded. And he doesn't appear all that wild...just sitting there holding a cane in his hands. From here she could see the lack of expression in his eyes, but no disfigurement. Myrtle Stinchcomb had explained that even though the boy had been with his father in the motor car accident, he was actually uninjured, himself. Except there was this blindness for which, as a German specialist said, there seemed to be no physical cause. Still the lad <u>was</u> blind!

Phoebe couldn't recall the name of the condition. It was a very long word over which even Myrtle Stinchcomb had stumbled. Something not yet fully understood, she confided, by the most skilled physicians.

"I can't see the beauty, Grandfather," the young voice had an edge of plaintiveness.

"Ah, yes, Robbie," the old man spoke regretfully. He reached his hand to pat the boy's shoulder. "But we shall keep hoping that it will be as the good Doctor Von Rottman says might happen; someday, at any time, your sight will return! You <u>must</u> believe that, dear boy!" he finished strongly.

Phoebe felt suddenly overwhelmed by a surge of deep sadness. She realized with honest uneasiness that it wasn't for this Robbie who lived in an elegant mansion, and despite the advantages of wealth, was blind.

No. It was for herself. For Phoebe Ogilvie. A poor little girl who had no kind grandfather to love her and speak encouraging words of comfort. <u>Why</u> should someone, <u>anyone</u>, have it all--Gardiner Hall, wealth, a loving grandfather?

After all, what is so bad about being blind? She eased back from the peep place, stepped away a few paces, squeezed both eyes closed. Walking around slowly she kept her bearings as she visualized the wall, the swing on the oak branch, the play table and box seats, and...

<u>Crack</u>! Her eyes flew open as her head hit the lowest branch of the tree. Letting out a yelp, she clapped her hand across her mouth stifling a cry of mixed pain, surprise, and insight. So <u>that</u> is why he carries that cane!

Rubbing her head she looked through the hole expecting to see both of them staring in her direction. Surely they heard the cry. But the old gentleman was talking about the tarts cook was making. The boy... the boy was facing the peep place with his head cocked to one side and a frown puckering his brow.

"What's over there, Grandfather? Is it still the cottage the Meachams had before we left?"

"Eh? Oh," his grandfather cast a quick glance, "yes, Robbie. We haven't taken on a new seamstress yet. And we hardly need a groomsman now. Remember I sold the stable. Just kept the one horse for your Uncle Esmond. You don't want a pony, do you?"

"No. I can't ride. Who lives there now? In the cottage?"

Phoebe wasn't prepared for the answer to that question.

"A young mother and her daughter leased it a while before we returned from abroad. A widow, I believe Mathers said. Keeping the place up nicely. Daniel Bacon is doing the handy work. Good man, Daniel Bacon."

It wasn't that an important man like Gavin Gardiner knew about her existence that mystified Phoebe. What was that he said about Mam? Young. Was Mam young? Phoebe thought her mam was pretty with her short curly hair, large grey eyes, and kind ways. Somehow she had never thought of Mam as young!

"Well, boy, are you ready to go back to the manor?" The old man looked off in the distance, speaking more to himself than his grandson. "We must do something about schooling. Soon."

Robbie gave an exclamation of alarm. "Not yet! Please, Grandfather, not yet. I want to get used to being at home." He pulled at the old man's jacket sleeve, resting his head pleadingly on a thin shoulder.

"There, there Robbie. Of course we'll wait until you're rested from all those travels and tests. Now! How about stopping off in the kitchen to beg a tart from Mrs. Wicker?" he propositioned with enthusiasm.

Robbie's face showed no eagerness. "No. I'd like to sit here and listen to the birds. Would you send Decker for me in a little while? I'll stay right here on the bench."

Gavin Gardiner hesitated. But with the boy's insistence that he would not budge until the valet came, his grandfather walked away slowly toward the manor.

Phoebe waited. A feeling, a strange spine-tingling feeling, seeped through her whole body. She suddenly knew, she was absolutely <u>sure</u> that the boy knew she was <u>there</u>: Well, not <u>her</u>. But <u>someone</u>.

He sat still. Very still. Holding her breath Phoebe picked up the stone intending to slide it back and be gone. She stopped, transfixed, when his voice rang out shrilly.

"<u>I know you are there</u>," he called out accusingly.

Phoebe's heart pounded furiously. She could feel a hot thumping in her ears.

"Who are you?" the voice grew stronger, tinged with impatience.

Phoebe felt a tingling wave of irritation. That one always gets what he wants, she thought. She was trying to make up her mind what to do: stand there waiting until he tired out and this Decker came to get him, or just walk away and leave him yelling. One thing was for sure, she would <u>not</u> answer!

"You are a <u>spy</u>! My grandfather worked in the Foreign Office against spies during the war. He <u>hates</u> spies!"

Stung with feelings of guilt, Phoebe bit her lip, cringing as the attack gathered steam.

"If it were wartime," Robbie's voice was now loud and venomous, "you would be <u>shot</u>! I shall tell my grandfather! He knows what to do with sneaks and spies! And that's what <u>you</u> are!"

Now fully aroused by the hateful assault, Phoebe could hold back no longer. Putting her mouth to the peep hole, she hissed, before ramming the stone back into place:

"And <u>you</u> are a <u>tattle-tale</u>! And <u>tattle-tales</u> have <u>no</u> friends!"

Chapter Four

Ats Offs and Thans

"You are going to do <u>what</u>?" Myrtle Stinchcomb stared at Mam incredulous.

Mam was unperturbed. "Today after lessons, we are going to call on the master at Gardiner Hall."

Mrs. Stinchcomb's mouth gaped still wider. "<u>Why</u>? For mercy sakes, Millicent, <u>why</u>?"

"It is the civilized thing to do," Mam said patiently. "We'll take some jars of strawberry jam and simply express our appreciation for living in this nice little cottage."

"Millie--Millicent--" Mrs. Stinchcomb floundered helplessly awash in frustration. "One doesn't go calling on people in <u>manors</u>! They are of better station in life and…"

"Nonsense," Mam interrupted gently. "They are people, ordinary people, who have joys and sorrows like the rest of us. Times are changing, Myrtle, and class isn't what it used to be."

"I would never, <u>never</u>, mind you, have gone to Gardiner Hall without a personal invitation from Lydia Gardiner! And even <u>then</u> I felt like I was in a place I didn't belong! Ambrose has talked many times with the old gentleman, and done considerable business through his manager, Adam Mathers, but we wouldn't go <u>calling</u>, like---like--" she sputtered, "<u>friends</u>!"

"Well, then, I think you were surely the loser. Lydia Gardiner was a lovely lady, no doubt. And I couldn't possibly live practically next door without making a social call," Mam said.

"Social call! My word!" Myrtle Stinchcomb fanned her face vigorously with her handkerchief. "My dear, this is the man who disowned a son for marrying out of his class! He does not receive people who happen to lease a cottage formerly used by staff! You are overstepping the boundaries of propriety, Millicent!" She wagged a finger warningly.

Phoebe listened, then left to hunt up Old Daniel. He was down on his knees weeding between the tender turnip plants. She sat cross-legged nearby, watching the gnarled hands pull the invaders up by the roots. His old cap perched jauntily on his gray head, and he hummed contentedly.

"Mr. Bacon, are some people better than other people?" she asked.

He sat back looking at her. Taking off his cap, he scratched his head, and Phoebe could tell he was thinking about it. Finally, clapping the cap back in place, he nodded, satisfied with his conclusion.

"Aye. But there be all kinds of better, lass. First you have your *ats*...better at working the soil, better at rugby, better at this and that."

Phoebe nodded. "But I mean..." she tried to remember something Mrs. Stinchcomb said. "Are some people in better stations than others? And what," she demanded, "are stations?"

"Ah now, lass, it's the *offs* you're speaking of there. You have your royals, your barristers, your gentry. Those folk with their lands and monies are better off than others, ye see.

"But now, ye asked about the *thans*. Is one person better than another? I don't hold to the idea of *thans*, lass. Those of us who are *ats* and *offs* know exactly why. The *thans* have a wee problem with that one." He settled back to his work as Phoebe pondered another nagging question.

Would the people at Gardiner Hall be *ats*, *offs*, or *thans*? Or maybe, *offs* and *thans*? She decided against asking Old Daniel, for he was leaving to get a hand spade from his lorry and worrying aloud about when to set out the tomato plants.

Wandering back to the house she glanced at the place where the honeysuckle covered the loose stone. What a horrid spoiled brat that Robbie is! Getting all upset because someone was looking, just looking through a hole. Shot indeed! His kind grandfather wouldn't have anyone shot just because Tattle-tale said so!

Yet, remembering how Robbie got his way about not starting lessons, and asking for this Decker person to come all the way from the manor to get him, and his whining about not being able to see the spring beauty, made Phoebe consider that the grandfather would do whatever Brat Robbie wanted! Somehow she couldn't help feeling a bit uneasy.

Phoebe entered the kitchen hoping Mam would treat her with a slice of the freshly-baked bread she could smell. Maybe a tart. Her mam was probably better at baking tarts than even the cook at Gardiner Hall! She smiled to herself. Old Daniel was a smart one, he was.

"Come Phoebe, time for lessons," Mam said.

Phoebe washed her hands before picking up the piece of cambric. She did not like sewing handkerchiefs, but Mam thought it to be a necessary task - part of learning genteel habits and skills. Someday, Mam told her, she would be needle-pointing and tatting. Mam patiently demonstrated over and over the rhythmic ease of accomplished stitching. Phoebe was proud that her own work was becoming neater with fewer stains from pricks.

Next came a lesson in reading, followed by sums, then conversation in French. Phoebe liked that. Mam had started her in French years ago, and promised that someday they would visit Paris. Imagine that! Across the Channel to Paris!

They would skip the history lesson today, Mam said, as she gathered up the books. Phoebe felt a stir of expectation. Something was going to happen. And she knew what it was before Mam spoke.

"We're going to wash up, put on our best, and make a call. To Gardiner Hall," Mam said, sounding like nothing out of the ordinary was taking place at all.

When they started out along the lane sometime later, Mam was wearing her fine cotton lawn and a hat whose broad brim flounced prettily as she walked, and Phoebe wore her blue muslin with the nice plaid sash. Phoebe had considered asking to wear her locket. But she decided not to bother Mam about getting it out.

Up the winding approach drive they walked. It was a mild April day, and Phoebe felt damp places popping out all over her face. She was going to wipe them away with her hand when Mam shook her head and handed her a lace handkerchief.

"Pat gently, Phoebe," she said. Phoebe did so, all the time thinking about the different ways people get rid of perspiration; some pat it away, some wipe it off, and some, like Myrtle Stinchcomb, fan it dry. The patters, the wipers, the fanners. She must remember to tell Mr. Bacon about that!

In front of the massive oak door at Gardiner Hall Mam smoothed Phoebe's hair and straightened her own skirt before lifting the bright polished knocker. The housekeeper, fingering a ring of keys, regarded them coolly.

Mam smiled, cleared her throat, and shifted the two jars of strawberry jam. "Good afternoon. My daughter and I are calling on Gavin Gardiner. Would he be receiving callers this day?"

They were studied even closer before the woman spoke. "Who is calling, please?"

"We are Millicent Ogilvie and daughter, Phoebe."

"Would you also be the tenants in the Meacham cottage?"

"We are."

"Are you sure you don't mean to talk with Adam Mathers, manager? His office is around back by the wellhouse. Just go..."

"No," interrupted Mam patiently. "We are calling on the master, Gavin Gardiner."

From behind the housekeeper a voice spoke up. "Who is it, Mrs. Lumley?" A woman came forward looking at Mam and Phoebe pleasantly. She was holding someone by the hand. Phoebe, seeing who it was, moved closer to Mam, feeling a bit unnerved.

"The tenant from the cottage, Madam. They are asking to see the master!"

Phoebe remembered the same hard edge of disapproval in Myrtle Stinchcomb's voice. She moved still closer to Mam.

"I'm Alice Lambert. Please come in."

Phoebe and Mam stepped inside the long hall on a floor polished and shining. Mrs. Lambert's pleasant manner comforted Phoebe somewhat.

"Thank you, Mrs. Lambert. I am Millicent Ogilvie, and this is my daughter, Phoebe. We do live in your cottage." Mam's gloved fingers held onto the jars of jam tightly.

"Father is in the library, Mrs. Ogilvie. Thank you, Mrs. Lumley," she dismissed the housekeeper with a nod.

"This is my son, Robbie," she said, putting the boy forward gently." "Robbie is unsighted at the present, but we hope for recovery any day," she patted the boy's shoulder. "Go along. The library is down the hall," she continued leading the way.

Phoebe looked at the portraits on both sides of the hall. They all seemed somber, rather unfriendly. All except the full-length portrait of the beautifully-gowned lady; slim, fair, with long brown tresses and soft eyes that smiled.

The library door was closed. Mrs. Lambert stood looking at it a bit uncertainly. She touched Mam's arm. "Mrs. Ogilvie, my father is...has been.." She stopped, a look of consternation moving across her face. "I'll step in a moment first..if you'll wait, please."

As they waited Mam strolled back up the hall looking at the portraits. Phoebe stood still, eyeing Robbie who faced her with those blank eyes that seemed to bore into her own.

"So <u>you're</u> the one," he spoke low, "who spies from the tenant house!"

Phoebe clenched her teeth. Was <u>this</u> what she got all dressed up for? To be insulted by this hateful, horrid mess of a *than*!

Chapter Five

The Threat

Gavin Gardiner was not alone. A man in a corner chair glanced up from his reading as they stepped into the room. Robbie's grandfather was at a desk, white head bent over papers. He continued writing until, after an embarrassingly long moment, Mrs. Lambert spoke.

"Father," she began.

Without raising his eyes, he held up a hand for silence.

Phoebe felt a chill, and looking up she saw Mam's pale face and trembling lips. Phoebe wished fervently they hadn't come to this place! Mam's idea of neighborliness wasn't a good one at all. If only I could whisper some magic words and be whisked away to making mud pies under the oak, Phoebe thought. Or be soaring high and free in the swing with the air ruffling through my hair. Or even back at the kitchen table having lessons with Mam looking contented instead of like she wants to cry.

The white-haired man finished writing, laid the pen aside, and raised his eyes to the four people standing just inside the door. Even from that distance, Phoebe could see the brown eyes were without warmth. Like those others who watched from the hall portraits.

Was this the same person she had seen and heard through the garden wall; the one whose gentleness, kindness, and soft words caused her to wish for just such a grandfather? Phoebe waited apprehensively as he beckoned with a thin hand.

"Father, as I just told you, this is Mrs. Ogilvie and her daughter, Phoebe, who have stopped in for a call on us." Mrs. Lambert smiled reassuringly at Mam, and then added, and this is my brother, Esmond Gardiner." She raised her voice so that the man reading looked up again. "Mrs. Ogilvie and Phoebe, Esmond."

He stood, bowing slightly. He was a tall man with a lean face, brown hair a bit shaggy, but not untidy. He looked at them frowning, then smiled cordially.

Phoebe thought she heard Robbie make a strange noise. Like a snicker. She looked at him quickly, but he wore the same expressionless mask.

"Mrs. Ogilvie," Gavin Gardiner rose also, motioning all of them to be seated. Mam sat, pulling Phoebe down beside her on the couch. Alice Lambert and Robbie settled together in a large leather chair. Esmond leaned against the wall, his arms folded loosely across his chest, and a scowl darkening his face once again.

"And now, would you have something to report about the cottage? Perhaps the roof leaks, or..."

"Father," Mrs. Lambert interrupted, plainly embarrassed by his cold, business-like manner.

At the same time, Mam, a warm pink spreading across her cheeks, came to life. She looked straight at Gavin Gardiner, her head high, eyes steady, unintimidated.

"Not at all, sir. The cottage is most comfortable. Our purpose is to speak as neighbors and present a culinary gift for your breakfast or tea enjoyment." She held out the jars of jam, and sat still, with no intention of walking across the distance between them.

They were staring at each other, and while the others present felt a definite challenge of sorts had been made, no one really understood who had made it. They might have remained frozen in that tableau forever, had not the younger Gardiner moved across the room to accept the offering.

"And a delicious addition to either one it will be. Thank you, Mrs. Ogilvie. And Phoebe." He looked down at Phoebe with such a nice smile she couldn't help smiling back. She suddenly felt <u>much</u> better.

Esmond Gardiner placed the strawberry jam on the desk before his father. "Your favorite, I believe you were saying just this morning," he said pleasantly.

"Yes," the older man replied. "Yes, it has been for many years, Esmond. And yours too, my boy. Your dear mother teased us both about our appetite for strawberry jam." For a moment his voice weakened, and he looked afar off as if playing a tantalizing game of hide and seek with memory.

Phoebe recognized his other self..that appealing person who was tender and caring. Just as suddenly he became controlled..coldly proper.

"Thank you for calling, Mrs. Ogilvie. Now, Alice," he waved a hand at Mrs. Lambert, "you will hostess for me in the garden. Please take tea before you leave, Mrs. Ogilvie." His nod was a clear dismissal. Something else was likewise as clear to Phoebe; Gavin Gardiner disliked them.

Alice Lambert rose with a sigh. Mam and Phoebe stood to leave the room. Esmond Gardiner waited at the door with an outstretched hand, and when Mam slipped hers into it, he smiled that very nice smile.

"It will be a pleasure to recall your visit, Madam," he said.

"And I your kindness, sir," Mam replied.

He stooped to take one of Phoebe's hands. "This has been a lovely day, Phoebe," he said gravely.

All the way outside Phoebe remembered his gentle ways. I <u>like</u> Esmond Gardiner, she thought, and he likes <u>us</u>.

In the garden Mrs. Lambert led them to a pretty picnic table and chairs. She directed a serving girl to bring tea.

"We'll let the children sit a moment while I show you my roses, Mrs. Ogilvie. Do you like roses?" She led Mam away as she chatted on about her climbers and tea roses. Would Mam like some cuttings? "Old

Daniel Bacon was known about Chestershire to be skilled at starting cuttings," she was reassuring Mam.

Phoebe settled down in a white wicker chair. Robbie sat swinging his leg vigorously, looking at her, yet not seeing. When he made a sound she recognized it as the same snicker she thought she heard earlier.

"What's funny?" she asked, trying not to sound cross.

"Him."

"Who?" Phoebe looked all around thinking he had heard someone walk up. There was no one else around.

"Him. In the library. My Uncle Esmond." He made the derisive sound once more.

"I think he's nice," Phoebe bristled.

"He's daft. Don't you know that? Can't remember a thing. Wouldn't even know his own name if he hadn't been told."

"That's not being daft," Phoebe said stoutly.

"That's what I call it," Robbie declared. "Whenever he meets someone, he gets a frown on his face like he's trying to remember something..he goes around frowning most of the time. My mother tells me," he added, just as Phoebe was about to ask how he knew this. "I'm blind, you know," he reminded her.

"So does that make you daft?" Phoebe inquired with feigned curiosity.

"What do you mean?" Robbie stopped swinging his leg, sitting up smartly.

"When a person has some kind of problem, like not being able to remember, or using a crutch, or being blind..does that mean they're daft?" she asked innocently.

"Of course not, stupid! They're just like other people! They can't do some things, but can others! Same as everybody else!"

"Oh." Phoebe gave a smug grin of satisfaction.

At that moment the serving girl approached and spoke to Robbie.

"*Est-ce que vous et notre jeune invite desirez des fruits avec du the, du pain et des sandwiches beurres?*" she asked quietly.

Robbie answered crossly. "Don't talk so fast, Monique. You know I can't understand unless you go slower. What about fruit?"

"She wants to know if we want fruit with the tea and sandwiches." Phoebe told him.

"*Quel genre de fruit?*" Phoebe stood up to speak to the girl who was plainly startled.

"*Des morceaux d'orange et de poires,*" Monique answered, looking at Phoebe with undisguised curiosity.

"What's she saying now?" Robbie demanded.

"*J'aimerai les deux et lui aussi.*" Phoebe smiled at the girl. "*Merci.*"

Monique left, casting an admiring glance at Phoebe.

Phoebe turned to Robbie. "I told her we both would like the orange and pear slices.

"How...where...who teaches you to speak French?" He was dumbfounded at what had just taken place.

Phoebe sat back down. She straightened her dress, smoothing the skirt carefully.

Impatiently the boy stood, stamped his foot, his face dark with the rage of embarrassment. "How can you speak French? You're just a..." he stammered.

"Spy!" Phoebe said with an exaggerated gruff voice. Since she wasn't really a mean-spirited person, Phoebe relented and told him the truth.

"My Mam teaches me. We have lessons every day."

"What lessons?" he demanded.

"Reading, sewing, sums, history, and French."

Robbie was silent. Phoebe felt a strange uneasiness as she watched a different expression move across his face. When he spoke, her worst fears of impending doom were realized.

"She shall teach me, also!"

Phoebe stared at him horrified. "No!" she was angry.

"Yes!"

They were both on their feet now, facing each other; Phoebe, feeling the ravages of hot hostility, and Robbie, radiating the wild exhilaration of ill-gotten bounty.

"No. Mam will not tutor you." Phoebe repeated firmly. "I shall tell her to not be your tutor!"

"And I shall tell my grandfather that I am ready for schooling. He wants me to have schooling soon. And I want your Mam to be my tutor. If she refuses, I shall tell my grandfather that I want you and your Mam to move out of the cottage! And my grandfather," he said triumphantly," always gives me what I want!"

Chapter Six

Robbie's Secret

On the way home Phoebe considered telling about Robbie's threat. But Mam was deep in thought, walking faster and faster, causing Phoebe to almost skip to keep up. The pace kept Phoebe's mind off everything except how the left slipper was rubbing her heel into a blister.

Mam must surely be put out at herself for calling at Gardiner Hall, Phoebe thought breathlessly. Going there like it was an acceptable thing to do had been a mistake. There would be <u>no</u> going back, Phoebe was sure of <u>that;</u> even if the boy's mother had tried to make them feel comfortable at tea.

Alice Lambert had chatted away as they nibbled at sandwiches and fruit. Mam had talked, too, seeming to enjoy the visit. Yet now on the way home, she was solemn and quiet. As for Phoebe, she was sure she would never forget those dreadful minutes in the library, with every person present wishing to be elsewhere..all except Esmond Gardiner who seemed relaxed and friendly.

It wasn't <u>their</u> presence, Phoebe felt convinced, that caused his knitted brow and frowns. Not really. The poor man appeared to be puzzled, befuddled, searching for answers to questions of which only he was aware. Phoebe felt only sympathy for him, for she knew it was as Robbie had said; when Esmond Gardiner meets people he wonders if he just might have known them somewhere in his forgotten past.

Robbie! That spoiled, bothersome boy! He thinks-- he truly <u>believes</u> he can get his way about everything! Well! He's going to find out that Phoebe Ogilvie isn't frightened of his threats! She felt better as she resolved to utterly, <u>utterly</u> ignore this Robbie person of Gardiner Hall. From this moment on, she vowed, she would not <u>speak</u> of him, <u>think</u> about him, and most certainly would <u>not</u> pull the stone out of the garden wall to <u>look</u> at him!

"Phoebe!" Mam had slowed down, and Phoebe realized gratefully that they were actually strolling along, "what did you and Robbie talk about? Don't you think he's a brave boy? Is he a happy child?"

Dismayed at having to break her solemn pledge so soon, Phoebe was slow to answer. "We talked about his Uncle Esmond," she said truthfully.

That satisfied Mam. She nodded. "I think," she said thoughtfully, "that he and his nephew are probably quite good friends. Close friends."

Another thing Mam was wrong about! However Esmond felt about his nephew, that boy, totally unsympathetic about his uncle's plight, was rather amused by it, thinking the man daft! Remembering Esmond Gardiner's kind words and gracious manner made Phoebe even more resentful toward that heartless nephew.

Old Daniel was loading tools in the lorry when they walked up the front path.

"Mr. Bacon, would you have any need for rose cuttings? Or is it not the right time to start cuttings?" Mam took off her flowery hat and pushed her hair back.

He turned around, looking at them with interest. "It's a good time, Missus. Aye," he nodded, "that space along the wall in front of the honeysuckle needs rose bushes."

Phoebe was startled at that idea. Rose bushes <u>there</u> with their prickles would keep her from looking through to see what was going on at the manor! Oh, well, hadn't she decided she didn't care what was happening to that person across the wall?

"Alice Lambert tells us you are known in Chestershire for skill in starting healthy bushes from cuttings," Mam went on. "She will give us as many as you're interested in using."

Old Daniel looked pleased as he considered the matter. "This be the lady of Gardiner Hall?"

"Yes. We--Phoebe and I--called there this afternoon and took tea with Mrs. Lambert and her young son, Robbie."

It was easy to see he was astonished. Just like Myrtle Stinchcomb. Why is it when everyone else knows we don't belong there, Mam is so stubborn and unconvinced? Now she's talking about going back for rose cuttings! Phoebe fidgeted with impatience.

"Along the wall sounds like the perfect place." Mam smiled. She moved toward the door calling back over her shoulder, "Come along, Phoebe. Change before you play."

Phoebe's gloomy lingering must have signaled her unrest to the old man's watchful eyes. "How was it, lass?" Old Daniel's sympathetic tone confirmed his suspicion.

Phoebe sighed. "Over there," she confided before walking away, "even the housekeeper is a better-than!"

It was two days later that Myrtle Stinchcomb came around. Just at teatime. Mam and Phoebe had put the books away and were getting tea things ready.

"Well," Mrs. Stinchcomb looked from one to the other expectantly, "what happened? At Gardiner Hall. Were you welcomed as you thought you would be?"

Giving a wry smile, Mam set the kettle on the stove. "More like you thought we would be, Myrtle," she admitted.

Mrs. Stinchcomb nodded understandingly. "I tell you, Millie," she said slowly, "when you spoke of times changing, I could almost agree, for I have seen it, myself, in the younger; a real desire to bring people together. But then, I've seen the older ones, still clinging to old beliefs like barnacles to a keel." She shook her head. "That's Gavin Gardiner. Up, down, back, forth, sideways, and ever which way!"

"You would think," she continued earnestly, "that anyone who has had the despair and sadness he has would have softened and feel... well, <u>humble</u>!"

Mam brought the kettle to the table and poured into the teapot. She looked at Phoebe, nodding toward the plate of scones on the cabinet. Phoebe carried the doomed cakes to the table, actually feeling quite kindly toward Myrtle Stinchcomb at the moment. There was something softer and more humble about even that outspoken lady. However, whereas her former attitude of outright disapproval of their Gardiner Hall visit seemed to have mellowed, her appetite had suffered no such moderation.

Phoebe put the plate on the table and drifted out back to the swing on the oak branch. At first she hadn't been all that enthused when Old Daniel put up that swing. Secretly she had the feeling she was too old for it. She quickly changed her mind. Since she couldn't climb the tree, at least she could sail through the air, feeling the thrill of being <u>up there</u>, free, yet attached, like a spider trailing a thread behind that anchors and secures its flight! That's what she did now, pushing off and pumping her legs to soar as high as the thick branches would allow.

Actually, if she really wanted to see anything over that wall, she had to take the stone out and - much as she detested Robbie's taunt - <u>spy</u>!

Of course, she had decided to never do that again. And after rose bushes were set out along the wall she wouldn't want to be scratched by thorns. And after all, she had already seen what was the most interesting; the transforming of an untended garden into clean curving lines of colorful borders, neatly pruned shrubs, and trimmed lawn.

The thought did enter her head now. Should she take just <u>one</u> more look through the peep hole? She knew she was going to, but the solemnity of the moment--this being the very <u>last</u> time and all-- persuaded her to let the swing slowly come to a standstill on its own. She sat there a long moment, looking down at a black beetle make a trail of tiny tracks in the dirt. It came to a rock and kept trying to climb over, falling back continually, until the last attempt caused the poor thing to flop over on its back and lay there waving its legs helplessly.

"If you can't get over something, you should go around it," she advised, flipping the creature over with a stick. She watched it scramble away with renewed strength.

When she looked through the peep place she saw two people walking slowly on a path. One was the valet, Decker, and the other was Robbie, tap-tapping with his cane. Wouldn't you know he would be arguing over something? Decker kept shaking his head. Robbie stopped, stamped a foot, and waved the cane in the air angrily. Just like that silly beetle, Phoebe thought.

Finally Decker appeared persuaded. He waited as the boy sat down in the shade of a small tree, then started back toward the manor casting several glances of uncertainty back over his shoulder.

Phoebe pressed her lips together with disgust. Got his way again! She watched Robbie as butterflies flitted about his head and over the shaggy asters nearby. A huge monarch, its wings drawn together rested on a grass blade.

Thunderstruck Phoebe stared as Robbie, leaning over, stealthily raised his hand, and moving ever so slowly, captured the butterfly between his thumb and forefinger! He held it up, looking closely at its wiggling legs, then flung it away to freedom!

Chapter Seven

Visitors

Truth was a lightning bolt crackling through Phoebe's brain with a shattering brilliance! She turned from the wall wide-eyed and shaken, the knuckles of a hand pressing hard against her teeth. When she remembered to breathe she almost strangled as she swallowed, trying to calm the turmoil ravaging her thoughts.

Robbie Lambert was not blind! It had already happened--what the doctors said might happen. Sometime--and no one but Robbie knew when--he had regained his sight!

He hadn't told anyone! He had his own selfish reasons for keeping news of the long awaited cure from his worried mother and grandfather, Phoebe was quite sure of that.

And that lie! She suddenly remembered that lie! About his mother telling him his Uncle Esmond frowns when he meets people. She remembered Robbie's snicker in the library. Now she knew certainly that no one told him about it. He had seen it! He could see everything for himself!

Why, he even knows where the stone comes out of the garden wall, she realized dumbfounded. Furthermore, she was thinking, he knows what I look like--and that thought, for some reason, nettled her terribly. Robbie Lambert is himself a spy of the worst kind! Condemns someone for doing the very thing he is doing himself!

So, why wouldn't he shout out his wonderful news, Phoebe puzzled. Why else except he gets his own way much easier with everyone feeling sorry for him? He has his mother, grandfather, uncle, Decker, and all the other household people giving in to him on all sorts of things! For one thing he gets out of being sent away to school. Oh yes, it's easy to understand why Robbie has kept his secret!

But she didn't have to keep it! Phoebe smiled, imagining how astonished Mam and Myrtle Stinchcomb would be when she told it right now! And with Mrs. Stinchcomb, it would be the same as telling all of Chestershire! Phoebe let out for the cottage feeling as if she would burst with excitement!

Somewhere along the rush up the path, another idea popped into her thoughts; is this the right time for telling?

Could this information be better used at another time? What if, she asked herself, Robbie keeps threatening me? It just might be wise to have a threat of my own. Her steps slowed and she stood still considering the situation. Yes, she decided, I shall keep this for a while, in case I need it for my own protection.

In spite of feeling a definite disappointment about holding her peace, Phoebe couldn't suppress an expression of satisfaction. She felt Mam look at her curiously at different times the next several days.

"You look," Mam said at one time, "like the cat that swallowed the canary." Noting Phoebe's wide-eyed innocence, she corrected herself. "No," she said softly, "like the canary that swallowed the cat!"

Phoebe smiled complacently. Even Old Daniel looked at her closely that week. She knew she was acting differently, like she had something on her mind, and she almost told Old Daniel what it was. But after letting several opportunities go by, the resolve to keep the secret became stronger than the urge to tell it.

If she had known that the first time she needed to use her weapon, she would be unable to do so, she might have confided in Old Daniel. Just to get his reaction. But Phoebe didn't tell.

Neither Mam nor Phoebe was prepared for the unexpected visitors who arrived several days later at teatime. When the bell at the front door sounded Mam sent Phoebe to answer. Phoebe wondered why Mrs. Stinchcomb who seemed to plan her visits for that time, didn't just walk in as usual.

But it wasn't Myrtle Stinchcomb. Through the lace curtains Phoebe saw the gleaming gray Bentley and the uniformed figure standing stiffly beside it. While pondering that, a movement through the front door glass brought her eyes to the man standing just beyond.

Phoebe trotted back to the kitchen standing speechless with a stricken look. Mam paused, teakettle in midair, looking at her.

"Phoebe? What is it?"

Phoebe swallowed. "It's him! Out there! It's him!"

Mam set the kettle on the stove. She untied her apron, straightened her skirt, patted her hair in place, and went to the parlor door.

There on the stoop standing straight and proper, was Gavin Gardiner. Beside him was young Robbie Lambert, staring vacantly.

"Good afternoon, Mrs. Ogilvie." He removed his hat courteously. "As you can see, Robbie and I are returning your call."

Mam, flushed and flustered, stepped back, opening the door wider. "Please do come in, sir. How nice to see you again, Robbie."

Phoebe watched Robbie stumble a bit as he moved inside sliding his feet along hesitantly. He can do it so well, she marveled. With just the right carefulness and mincing steps. And his eyes. They appeared glazed, sightless, looking over, under, around things. Never at anything! He was so good at playing the game no one would ever guess it was an act.

After seating them in the parlor Mam excused herself and Phoebe to bring in the tea tray. Phoebe helped gather things together and followed behind as Mam wheeled in the serving cart.

"This is kind of you, Mrs. Ogilvie, Most kind." Gavin Gardiner accepted a cup of tea. Phoebe watched Robbie hold out his hands waiting for someone to place a cup in them. Mam did, gently guiding his fingers to the handle. Phoebe fumed inside, knowing what the slight smile on his face meant; he was playing someone for a fool and enjoying their ignorance.

"Mrs. Ogilvie," Gavin Gardiner looked at Mam, speaking smoothly, "my daughter tells me that I was not at all cordial when you called at the manor last week."

Mam picked up the plate of scones, but he waved it away. "My son, Esmond, says quite bluntly, that I was rude. I'm curious, Madam, what would your opinion be of my behavior?"

"I think, sir, somewhere between the two. But, no matter," Mam smiled at him pleasantly, "I took no offense."

"Yes. Well, Madam, I do offer apology for whatever lack of civility I displayed."

Mam bowed her head in acceptance of his remark.

"And," he went on, " to speak with you about a certain matter. A business matter." He set the cup down. "As you know, my grandson, here, is sightless." He rested his hand on the boy's shoulder. "The accident happened when he was six years of age. Robbie witnessed his father's death in the motor car accident, and was trapped himself for some time before being rescued. The doctors say his sight could return at any time, and we, of course, pray daily for that blessing."

Mam murmured sympathetically, and Phoebe swallowed hard, hating the feeling that she was somehow sharing Robbie's hypocrisy.

"Madam," he continued, "due to his young age Robbie had very little tutoring before the accident. And none since. As we wait for sight to return he has little mental stimulation. I find it difficult to consider sending him away for schooling while in such defenseless, and vulnerable circumstances."

Phoebe sat up straighter, hardly daring to breathe. She <u>knew</u> what Gavin Gardiner was there to do! She thought wildly of dragging Mam out of the room, into the kitchen, to warn her of what was going to be requested!

Why, oh, why hadn't she told Mam about Robbie's threat? And Mam should know that he is <u>not</u> blind! He's a mean-spirited, spoiled boy who lies, calls Phoebe names, and threatens her! But now, it's too late to warn Mam about any of this! She's sitting there completely unprepared for the disaster Phoebe knew was about to happen!

"Robbie tells me, Mrs. Ogilvie, that you conduct daily lessons for Phoebe."

Mam looked taken back for a moment, then answered simply. "Yes."

"Would you consent to include Robbie in those lessons?"

Mam's mouth dropped open a bit and she stared at Gavin Gardiner. In the silence following the abrupt question Phoebe remembered that other time in the Gardiner Hall library when only another's gentle intervention had resolved an awkward moment between these two. But there was no Esmond this time to smooth over a confrontation.

Mam found her voice. "You cannot be serious, sir. Surely not. How can I teach Robbie? I--I--have no training..I know nothing of methods for teaching blind children." She raised a hand helplessly, shaking her head. "I cannot. Really sir, I cannot be considered qualified for such a task."

"Nonsense," he said brusquely. "I do not agree. It's easy to see, Madam, that you do well indeed. I understand that your daughter speaks French well. Her excellent demeanor testifies to your qualifications, I might add."

"Robbie is a bright lad. He will learn quickly regardless of methods. And I must tell you, Mrs. Ogilvie, this is the desire of the boy, himself. He is keen on the idea of beginning studies. His mother is overjoyed at his enthusiasm."

"Now, about the business matter." He was giving Mam no opening to protest further. "There is a schoolroom on the third floor of Gardiner Hall that needs using. You can hold classes in it for both children as did the tutors for Esmond and Alice years ago." His eyes roved the room critically. "Your own rooms there will be every bit as comfortable as these." His gaze moved back to meet Mam's startled one. "More so, I dare say."

"You mean..." Mam began uncertainly.

"Exactly. I want to employ you, Madam, as tutor for my grandson. And as such, it will be advisable for you and Phoebe to live at Gardiner Hall!"

Chapter Eight

Leaving the Cottage

Gavin Gardiner talked on about how the schoolroom would be freshened and made ready; new drapes were most definitely required, the globe, bent against the frame from a long-ago tumble off a desk, was doubtful, and the old desks, at least Esmond's, were scarred from his practicing with a Christmas knife when he was eleven.

"He was an industrious lad," he chuckled, "and not always at the right task."

Phoebe looked at Mam. She will speak up again, of course. Mam will say no again. If he would just stop talking she would say no. No, but thank you. That's what she would say. Phoebe was sure of it.. until she realized Mam was listening. Really listening. Feeling a twinge of uneasiness, Phoebe stole a sideways glance at Robbie.

She didn't like the way his thin lips were pressed together in a pleased smirk. This whole thing is his doing, she fumed inside.

When Robbie spoke, his rising voice sounding earnest and appealingly timid, Phoebe winced in disgust.

"I would be so grateful, Madam, if you would consent to be my tutor. You would be pleased at my progress for I would try very hard."

Now was a time that Mam could express doubt and reluctance! Phoebe sucked her breath in, waiting hopefully. But she slumped in disappointment as Mam's hand reached over to gently pat Robbie's shoulder.

"Of course you would, Robbie. I'll think about this very carefully I promise," Mam told him.

She looked at Gavin Gardiner. "I will consider the matter, sir. Carefully. I wonder.." she hesitated a moment before continuing. "Would it be possible for us to remain here in the cottage? We're settled in quite comfortably and.."

He dismissed the idea with a raised hand and shake of his head. "No. No, not practical at all. We'll be hiring more household staff shortly and the cottage will be needed. I believe Stinchcomb made that possibility clear, did he not?"

"So, you think on this business, Madam, and send word to the manor when you know your mind on the matter. And now, Robbie," he stood, picked up his hat, and took the boy's arm, "let us return home and leave Mrs. Ogilvie to make her decision. The right one, I am sure."

And so, Phoebe thought gloomily, watching them climb into the handsome Bentley, there is not much difference between the two of them; both grandfather and grandson want their own way and are not above scheming to get it! Robbie had made good on his threat, she conceded. Yet, clever and conniving though he was, Phoebe felt his grandfather as much to blame, bending to the whims of that spoiled willful boy!

Perhaps Mam would surprise them both! After all, there just might be some other cottage to let in Chestershire by now! Ambrose Stinchcomb did say there could be something available later.

Phoebe hurried into the kitchen where Mam was pumping water into the kettle for heating. "Mam, I don't want to...," she began resolutely, but stopped as Mam turned around. Mam's face was aglow, her eyes shining so that Phoebe gaped in bewilderment... "to go," she finished weakly.

Mam put the kettle on the stove and turning, she studied Phoebe a long moment. "To Gardiner Hall, you mean?"

Phoebe nodded, blinking hard to keep tears from spilling out of her eyes. Mam sat down and pulled her close. "Well," she began reasonably, "it is a truly beautiful house, dear. Wouldn't you really like to live in as grand a house as Gardiner Hall?"

Phoebe shook her head vigorously. "Not like here. We have the cottage fixed just the way we like it," she said stubbornly.

"Yes. But Phoebe," Mam pointed out patiently, "You heard what was said. We can't stay here much longer anyway. We're going to have to move whether we go to Gardiner Hall or not."

"And that's not the first time I heard that either!" Phoebe exploded.

Mam stared at her. "Whatever do you mean?" she asked quietly.

And so Phoebe told. All about Robbie Lambert from the very first. About the loose stone in the wall. About Robbie calling her a spy and saying she could be shot. About his Uncle Esmond being daft. About being the spy from the tenant house. And finally about his threat made that day in the Gardiner Hall garden as they waited for tea.

"He said he would tell his grandfather he wanted you for his tutor, and if you refused they would make us move," she said, "and he did and they are!" she finished.

Mam pushed Phoebe's hair back from her forehead gently, brushed a tiny sugar speck from her upper lip. "Phoebe, it may be as it seems, that this boy is spoiled and unkind. There's something else we must consider just now. The time will come when I must think about some kind of work. Dada's and my savings won't last forever. And being a tutor is far better than a shop clerk. I'll be paid well, you and I will be together, and in a household like Gardiner Hall, only the housekeeper is more respected, among all the staff. Just think, we'll have our own rooms, probably a suite of rooms!"

"I understand another worry you have now...trouble between you and Robbie. But remember, I'll be there to see you aren't bullied." Mam smiled encouragingly. "I have a problem, too," she said. "How am I going to tutor a boy with no sight?"

Phoebe smiled. Now she could share the Big Secret! She told Mam what she had seen through the peep place as Robbie caught the butterfly and looked at it closely before throwing it up to freedom. Mam listened quietly, not interrupting.

"He's a rascal," she said finally, "a real little actor."

"You'll tell Robbie's mother and grandfather, won't you, Mam? They'll be so happy, won't they?"

"I'm sure they would be overjoyed," Mam agreed. "But no," she shook her head. "We won't be telling them or anyone, Phoebe."

"Why not?" Phoebe demanded. "It would pay him back for his hatefulness to me!"

"<u>That's</u> why we aren't telling, dear. A motive for revenge isn't a reason for doing anything. When you know something, you have to be willing to accept responsibility for whatever happens if you tell the thing. Robbie has not told this good news to the people who love him very much. Now, will it do them good to learn of that? Or is it best to let events unfold without our meddling...and not be responsible for whatever changes in lives and feelings might come following the telling?"

Mam wrote a note of acceptance and asked Old Daniel to deliver it to Gardiner Hall the next day. An answer came by messenger the next morning requesting Mam to have things ready for transporting on Friday. A lorry would be sent at three o'clock that afternoon.

Phoebe moped about cheerlessly. She followed Old Daniel about as he chopped weeds. Would he keep coming to the cottage?

"Aye. Ye needn't fret about that, lass. The master sent word I'm to keep to the job. He wants the place kept spiffy neat."

Would she ever see him again? "Aye. Sometimes Avery Baskin wants help pruning and I give him a hand. I'll see you when you least expect Old Daniel is anywhere abouts!"

Phoebe was cheered at hearing that. She even felt anxious that Myrtle Stinchcomb find out where they were going. If she had felt happier about what was happening herself, Phoebe would have enjoyed that lady's reaction later that day.

Myrtle listened to Mam's news, her mouth dropping open, sitting so still she seemed hypnotized. She said not a word when Mam finished and waited for some response.

"Myrtle," Mam said in a worried voice. Mrs. Stinchcomb blinked her eyes, started to speak, but no sound came out. She swallowed, moistened her lips, swallowed again.

"Myrtle," Mam shook her gently. "Are you all right?"

She nodded. Mam said how nice it was all going to be, how interesting to be a gentry tutor, and how Myrtle must come for tea. Often.

Finally recovering somewhat, Myrtle offered good wishes, assuring Mam she truly would come to tea some afternoon. She departed, still in rather a daze over what seemed to be quite remarkably unbelievable events!

The several days left were spent in packing and leaving the cottage neat. On Friday they stood in the parlor waiting for the lorry. Around them they felt the melancholy air that seeps into uninhabited houses. Phoebe felt downcast and sad at leaving the little house.

At the precise moment they heard the lorry clattering down the lane, an idea shot through Phoebe's thoughts. She turned, dashed out the door, calling back over her shoulder, "I forgot something!"

Around the corner she sped. Down the path, to the garden wall behind the honeysuckle. Reaching through, her fingers dug out the loose stone.

"There," she said, laying it down out of sight behind a bush.

Chapter Nine

A New Home

The ride to Gardiner Hall seemed much longer to Phoebe than when she and Mam walked the distance. Had it been only two weeks since they came along this shady lane after calling at the manor? In some ways that visit was vague and shadowy, like the flitting fragments of an almost forgotten dream. But in others, stark memories made the whole thing quite genuine; that somber walk between the portraits on the walls, those chilling moments in the library, and Robbie's menacing declaration in the garden. Thinking about all of that, and how it was ending in this unreal departure from the cottage, Phoebe only half-listened to Mam and the driver talking as the lorry rattled along the narrow road.

"My Audrey says the old schoolroom is to be all fixed up for Master Robbie and your young one," he bent over to look across at Phoebe. "Now, that's good news to us service people for a fact. The lad needs teaching about a heap of things. Indeed he does!" He took his eyes from the road and fixed them on Mam. "Do you teach children how to behave?" He asked.

Mam smiled. "That is part of their schooling, Mr.---"

"Hardow. William Hardow. I'm probably what used to be called a footman at the manor, though nowadays we're just as handy at doing outside as in. My Audrey was actually a nursery maid at her last service, but she's housemaid at Gardiner Hall. No nursery here at this manor. Nor ever likely to be, seems."

He turned the lorry into the manor drive and hopped out to close the iron gate after they drove through. Climbing back in he went on talking. "The boy, Robbie," he shook his head, "kicked my shins during one of his mean streaks. Can't blame <u>that</u> on being blind, I say!"

"And I, too," Mam agreed sympathetically.

"Well, that's the young man's fancy; make life miserable for anyone who has to do with him and hide behind his blindness." He looked at Mam with undisguised pity. That one will be a hard one to teach."

"Yes," Mam agreed solemnly.

The lorry stopped at the front entrance and William Hardow set their boxes and valises at the front door. "I was told by Mrs. Lambert to bring you in this way," he said as Mam looked at him uncertainly.

Mrs. Lumley answered the bell. "Good day mam. Mrs. Lambert is in the drawing room. Hardow will take your things to your rooms on the second floor. "Phoebe was relieved at the more charitable tone of voice and a softening about her lips that was close to a slight smile.

Mam and Phoebe followed the housekeeper into the long, spacious room, beautifully furnished with brocaded chairs, settees, and polished tables centered with vases of garden flowers. Phoebe stared at the rich tapestries hanging on the walls beneath the high ceiling. It was a magnificent room, alive with the mellow air of exquisite elegance. Alice Lambert rose from a chair, hurrying across the room smiling a welcome to them.

"This is such a fine opportunity for my son, Mrs. Ogilvie. "She held out her bands and grasped Mam's gratefully. "Robbie is so pleased, I must tell you...and anxious to learn. Although, I know," she confessed, "that it will be a difficult task in many ways."

"I shall do my best," Mam said simply.

"Of course you will. Father and Esmond have Robbie with them at a land management meeting. They go to such things with Mr. Mathers. You know," she smiled ruefully, "Robbie has wasted time, valuable time, just following along to fill up his time. How wonderful it will be for him to have real purpose in his days!"

"Now, I'll show you to your rooms. Then if you like, we'll go up to the schoolroom. Come along."

Out into the hall again, past the library, they saw again the portrait of the beautiful fair lady with the smiling eyes. Without realizing it, Phoebe's steps slowed until she came to a complete stop, staring up at the painting. Mam and Alice Lambert turned back and stood with her.

"My mother," Mrs. Lambert said softly. "It was painted soon after my brother, Esmond, was born. She was much younger than Father, but they were devoted to each other."

"A lovely, kind lady," Mam murmured.

Alice Lambert looked at her appreciatively. "Oh, yes, Mrs. Ogilvie, she was indeed."

They walked on, Mam taking Phoebe's hand, pulling her along gently.

Upstairs a few moments later they followed Alice Lambert into a good-sized sitting room. There was a fireplace with a deep-cushioned couch in front of it, a desk, a round table with two chairs, a smaller table with a bowl of flowers in its center, and a big bay window with a padded seat beneath. Phoebe knew she would love sitting there.

"Through here is your bedroom," Mrs. Lambert led them through a door into a room with a huge, canopied four-poster bed. Hardow had already left their belongings in the recessed closet that stretched across one end of the room. Mam laughed outright, saying what a small part of it would be needed.

"Would you like to see the schoolroom?" Mrs. Lambert asked.

Mam said yes she would like that very much, and Phoebe nodded. She was still benumbed by the idea that gentry actually had a special room in their homes where children were tutored. A rough kitchen table had always been good enough for her and Mam.

Up another flight of stairs they climbed, onto the third floor. "We have a storeroom up here, just an attic room, really," Mrs. Lambert nodded toward a closed door. "And these two other rooms are used by housemaids. The schoolroom is at the end of the hall. Here we are." She opened the door and they stepped inside a big room, empty except for desks pushed together in a corner, a table bearing a clutter of hand slates, and a globe that leaned crookedly in its frame.

Their footsteps echoed sharply on the wood floor as they walked across to the dormer windows. "It's rather cheerless, I'm afraid," Alice Lambert said. "Father has ordered carpet and new slates, and a stand of new maps. Just about everything is out of date on this old thing," she twirled the globe and they watched it wobble drunkenly in its sprained orbit.

"The shape of it would be useful for Robbie's understanding," Mam said.

Alice Lambert looked at her in surprise. "Why yes, it would. We'll see if Hardow can straighten the poor thing. I know it's foolish, Mrs. Ogilvie, but I discouraged Father from replacing the desks. I do so want Robbie to use the one I had as a child." She pulled two desks out of the corner.

Mam picked up a piece of cloth from under the slates and vigorously dusted the desks. Both showed the usual marks of childish boredom, but the larger one, more so; up by the ink well was a deeply-carved crowned head, with the words, KING ESMOND, cut below it.

Phoebe walked over to one of the windows. There were three dormer windows along the wall. She looked down to the small garden place where she and Robbie had sat. Farther out from the manor stretched the back lawn, the view interrupted by the sycamores. Somewhere out there beyond the trees was the wall that ran past the cottage. And in that wall, at a certain place, was the hole. Soon..the very first chance she had..she would go there and peek through. Maybe she could see Old Daniel working, perhaps even talk to him.

Suddenly she realized someone had spoken to her. There was that kind of silence that follows an unanswered question, and she knew with hot embarrassment that an answer from her was expected.

"Mrs. Lambert wonders if you like the schoolroom, dear," Mam said.

"Yes. It's quite nice. Will it be cold in winter?" This question came from nowhere. She hadn't even wondered about such a thing. But Alice Lambert seemed pleased to point to the floor grates along the walls.

"When fires are laid below the heat comes up and makes this room as cozy as you could want. And on warm days the windows bring in lovely breezes."

She left them at their sitting-room door a few moments later. "I know you need time to get settled," she smiled.

Mam put the valises on the bed. She shook out garments, put them on hangers, and Phoebe stood on a box to reach the closet rod. They put Dada's leather book bag on a high shelf, and Phoebe realized how much lighter it had grown in the past months.

When a knock sounded at the door Mam opened it to a small figure in cap and apron. "Please, mam, I'm Audrey. Cook says you and the young miss are to eat now with staff. I'm to show you the way." She shifted self-consciously back and forth clearly uncertain whether or not this new household member required a curtsey. Later she was to mumble her bewilderment to Cook. "Eating with staff means one thing, Wicker, but glory be, this one looks as much a real lady as the master's own daughter!"

Mam and Phoebe followed the housemaid down the back stairs, winding around corners, through doors, past high windows letting shafts of daylight into the dark passageway.

Phoebe suddenly remembered something. As the slight figure ahead disappeared through a swinging door, she pulled Mam to a stop and whispered.

"Did you notice on the portrait? Around her neck? It's a locket exactly like mine."

Mam nodded. "Yes," she said. "Exactly."

Chapter Ten

Robbie's Mistake

Beyond the swinging door Phoebe and Mam stepped into the big kitchen, bright with hanging copper pans. Pots bubbled under clattering lids on the huge iron stove, and delicious smells drifted from ovens. They stood looking back at the group of people staring at them curiously. Strangely Phoebe felt no discomfort.

It was Cook, plump and dimple-cheeked, who rallied them all around for introductions, and starting with herself, gestured to each with a ladle. "I'm Wicker. You've met Audrey.." the housemaid smiled shyly. "This is Trevor who helps Mathers with the books, Monique there is serving girl." Phoebe remembered her from that other visit. "Della here also serves and cleans. Maggie, the laundress is visiting her mother. This here is Baskin, gardener, Hardow you've met, and this.." she ended as a tall spare figure entered from another door, "is the master's man, Decker."

Phoebe recognized him. He was taller up close than when she watched him walking with Robbie that time. And older. His face was long, his hair thin, and his shoulders were a bit stooped.

He looked at them without speaking for a long moment, then inclined his head to Mam in such a quiet dignity that Audrey felt better about her own awkwardness when meeting Mam the first time. "He held himself so grand," she whispered to Della later as they cleaned hearths, "like he was meeting the mistress of the house, herself!"

"Decker is valet, silver cleaner, and," Wicker winked mischievously, "butler..when he can beat Lumley to the door!" An appreciative burst of laughter followed, and in the companionship of the moment, Mam and Phoebe felt a warm sense of belonging.

"I am Millicent Ogilvie. And this is Phoebe. I am to tutor young Robbie," Mam smiled.

"And none too soon. None too soon," Wicker nodded. "Now," she motioned to the long table flanked on both sides by benches, "let's get to this shepherd's pie and steamed ginger pudding before the family needs serving!"

Getting settled at Gardiner Hall turned out to be easier than Phoebe thought it would be. The schoolroom was being restored with fresh paint, the floor re-varnished even though carpet was to be laid, new drapes were being sewn, and study supplies ordered. While they waited for all this to be done, and afterwards for the room to air from odors, Mam conducted class on garden benches or in the gazebo. She had cautioned Phoebe again about ignoring Robbie's blindness sham. It would be revealed, she said, when its time had come.

And so Mam lectured on nature, history, conducted conversations in French, helped Robbie identify money pieces by size and shape, and kept Phoebe busy with her cambric handkerchief handwork.

At teatime Robbie quickly discovered Mam would brook no display of crude manners. "The gentlemanly procedure, Robbie," she stilled his hands from groping across the tray for scones," is to allow the ladies to serve and be served first."

He turned his head in Phoebe's direction, bad-tempered and unconvinced. "All the ladies," Mam said firmly, passing the tray to Phoebe, receiving it back, then guiding Robbie's hand to his plate. "Now I'm pouring tea. First the ladies. Then, your cup by your right hand, Robbie." Calmly and persistently he was held to waiting to be properly served, and to offering such genteel expressions of "if you please," and "thank you."

After taking tea with them the first time his mother was impressed. "We have overlooked many things in these past few years since the accident. Many things." She shook her head regretfully. "In a way we were as blind as Robbie. If he resisted doing something, whether acting mannerly or whatever, we just felt sorry for him. Overlooked and excused him." Her eyes misted over and she shook her head again.

Robbie wasn't all that reformed, Phoebe knew; twice he kicked her legs as they sat in the gazebo, once while she was reciting the Beatitudes. Once he leaned over to whisper "tenant girl" while Mam was discussing the Houses of Parliament.

When the schoolroom was ready Phoebe moved her desk as far from his as Mam allowed. She was thrilled he had not wanted his Uncle Esmond's desk with the beautiful crowned head carved in it. He made a great show of running his hands all over the desk tops, tracing marks and grooves, finally announcing his choice.

"Not this old thing," he pushed it away scornfully. "Someone ruined it with all that carving."

Knowing that he thought them fools, Phoebe could hardly bear to be a part of the pretense. It didn't bother Mam one bit. "You've chosen your mother's desk, Robbie. She will be pleased of that." Mam said pleasantly.

Life at Gardiner Hall was actually comfortable. The one thing Phoebe missed was talking with Old Daniel. She hadn't realized how much she looked forward to meeting him in the mornings, watching him climb down from his lorry, unload his tools, and following him about just talking. Sometimes at the schoolroom window she fancied she caught a glimpse of him on the other side of the wall.

But then it was such a long way across the lawn back to the cottage, and the sycamores were so tall and leafy she could never be really sure. In the back of her mind she treasured the thought that the first chance she had, when she was alone, she would peek through that hole in the wall. She just might be able to talk to Old Daniel!

Phoebe was certain no one had moved into the cottage. It had all been a plot to get Mam to agree to tutoring Robbie Lambert, she thought darkly.

Mam, herself, seemed content. She rose each morning, teased Phoebe into a smile, managed Robbie's moods with no visible disruption to her own even disposition, and soothed any staff grumbler with a cheery greeting.

And she didn't even <u>look</u> the same, Phoebe noticed. She was letting her hair grow, brushing it back from her face and caught with a ribbon that matched her dress. "This is the way your dear Dada liked it, Phoebe," she said.

One evening as they sat before the fireplace in their sitting room Mam said, "I do believe it's time for Robbie to begin exercising. He does nothing to develop his muscles and strength."

The idea puzzled Phoebe. "How can he have exercise? He can't run or do anything as long as he pretends he can't see where he's going?"

"Well, I believe I have thought of a way," Mam said.

Robbie was upset. "I <u>cannot</u> see," he argued. "I would run into things, of course!" The three of them were sitting on the bench beside the small fish pond.

"Of course," Mam agreed patiently, "<u>if</u> you were alone. But I have thought of a way to make it work. You shall have an anchor so to speak. Here," she held a short piece of rope in her hands and pressed one end into his hands.

"You'll hold the end of the rope, Robbie. Someone else will hold the other end. You will run together across the open lawn where there are no obstacles. Your guide will go only in absolutely clear places."

He was not convinced.

"Let me show you, Robbie. I shall be your guide runner. You hold your end of the rope. Now let's move out slowly, let's trot. Don't fear."

Phoebe watched as they ran off, Mam putting on as good an act as Robbie, encouraging him to run and giving enthusiastic praise. Back they came to where Phoebe sat watching.

"That was fine, Robbie. Fine! You're going to like it! And it's so good for you to exercise your muscles!" Mam and Robbie were both breathless from running and laughing. Mam handed her end of the rope to Phoebe.

Phoebe looked at it disagreeably. Now I'm going to have to go through the same silly business with him. She looked at Mam pleadingly. But Mam sank down on the bench smiling.

"Now Phoebe, your turn to be runner guide. Not too far out. We don't want to tire Robbie out this first time. He needs to build up his endurance slowly."

Resigned, Phoebe tugged at the rope and off they trotted. Robbie was into the spirit of the game, running alongside with no hesitation now. She was amazed as always at his practiced blindness.

Across the broad lawn they ran. The whole thing suddenly seemed so ridiculous to Phoebe that she determined to take the little hypocrite back immediately. He was laughing now, and she felt hot with his mockery of the situation. Her anger made her almost blind to their closer and closer approach to the fish pond. Up ahead she did see Mam stand up, her eyes widening in alarm.

Robbie stopped laughing, slowed up, and halted to an abrupt standstill. Phoebe looked down, horrified to see they were only a few steps from the pond. She felt the rope yanked out of her hand, and turned to see Robbie's face contorted by fury. He was sputtering with outrage. Winding the rope into a tight coil he threw it violently into the water.

Marching to Mam, he stood, drawn up into a tight, shaking, hand-clenched specter. Pointing back to Phoebe he screeched, "<u>Did you see that? She was leading me straight toward the fish pond</u>!"

Mam stared at him. Too late Robbie realized his mistake.

Mam spoke first. "Yes, Robbie, I saw. And so," she went on softly, "did you!"

Chapter Eleven

Buried Guilt

Neither Phoebe nor Mam was prepared for what followed. They looked on in shock as Robbie slumped to the ground with a wild cry of despair, his fists beating a furious tattoo on the grass, his body shuddering with harsh sobs.

It was frightening to Phoebe, standing there staring at this eruption of raw agony, all the time struggling with uneasy thoughts about herself; was she innocent of malicious intent? Had she subconsciously tried to put him in harm's way? She had been thinking heatedly about all the implications of his continued deception, true. But to deliberately cause Robbie bodily harm? <u>Oh no</u>!

"I wasn't paying attention," she whispered. "I wasn't trying to hurt him."

"Of course you weren't," Mam squeezed her reassuringly. "There's no harm done. And who knows, maybe some good. Here, Robbie," she bent over and scooped the boy into her arms. Pulling him over to the bench, she held him, waiting--his body writhing and twisting--for the tantrum to subside. He struggled to be free, all the time the loud wailing, an unearthly keening, caused Phoebe to press both hands over her ears. She was shaken by the brute force of such misery.

Robbie was crying words; words that were garbled and muffled against Mam's shoulder. After a while Mam held him away, peering into his face.

"What is it, Robbie? What is really making you so unhappy? Please tell me," she urged. "Please trust me, Robbie!"

He wept all the harder, gasping for air. "I--I--was--caught, and couldn't get my arms out, and--he begged me to--help him! I couldn't move! I couldn't move! I couldn't help him!"

The words made no sense to them. He kept sobbing the same thing over and over, words that had no bearing on this moment.

Then suddenly, amid his agonized cries, understanding moved across Mam's worried face. "Dear God," she murmured, enfolding him close again, "he's remembering the accident all those years ago!"

She began to speak to him, raising her voice over his own so that he couldn't help but hear what she was saying.

"I understand, Robbie. I know," she said. "You're saying your father was hurt, and needed help. He asked you to help. You wanted so much to help him. And you couldn't. No matter how much you wanted to help your father, you couldn't."

She felt his head nodding vigorously against her cheek. "You were so young then, weren't you? You wanted to lift that heavy thing off, but you couldn't even lift it off of yourself: That's the way it was."

Another nod. Then his voice rose shrilly. "And there was blood! My father's blood! And he moved--as much as he could--and kissed me! He wasn't mad at me!" Another burst of sobs shook him.

Tears were running clown Mam's face. Holding him close, rocking gently back and forth, she felt the boy gradually quieting, sagging against her, exhausted, spent.

"Robbie, listen to me very carefully. Your father wanted you to know that he understood. He knew, remember this, Robbie, he knew you would have helped him if you possibly could have. And he kissed you to tell you so, and that he loved you, oh so very much!"

Robbie stepped back wiping tears with the back of his hand. "When they found us, I didn't know it. When I woke up, I couldn't see!"

Mam nodded. "But now you can." She patted his wet cheeks with her handkerchief. "When did your sight return?"

"In a London hotel lobby on our way home from France. Grandfather and Uncle Esmond left me sitting while they stepped to the desk. Some men passed and stopped close to me, talking. One of them," his voice broke, "sounded like my father! His cigar smelled like the ones my father smoked! I raised my face to smell it, and I could see the man! But it <u>wasn't</u> my father. <u>It wasn't him</u>!" He began to weep softly again.

It seemed an eternity to Phoebe before the crying eased into hiccoughing snuffles. She was feeling a strange stirring of pity for Robbie Lambert. Somehow he didn't seem the same hateful boy.

Mam straightened his collar, smoothed his clothes. "Everything will be all right, Robbie. Everything is fine. It's a good thing that we know you can see. You'll be glad someone knows. And this other thing that has bothered you won't hurt as much, because you have needed to talk about it. And you'll want to talk about it more with others who love you, and can help you understand about it even better than you do now."

"<u>But she tried to make me fall</u>!" She thought I couldn't see where she was leading me!"

Phoebe felt the heat of his accusing eyes.

"She--she," Robbie sputtered. "She already knew you could see. Phoebe has known that for a long time," Mam said quietly.

He looked at Phoebe disbelieving.

She nodded. "I saw you catch a butterfly, look at it, and watch it fly away."

He considered that with a knit brow. "That was before you came to Gardiner Hall," he said.

"I saw," Phoebe said, "through the wall." He looked at her scornfully. Turning to Mam he asked, "You knew, too?"

"Yes."

"Why didn't you tell?"

Mam shrugged. "You're the one to do the telling, Robbie."

"Hello there! What's happening with lessons today?" They were startled to hear the voice and see Esmond Gardiner striding toward them. He was wearing jodhpurs, probably on his way to the stable. He squatted in front of Robbie, looking into his face intently.

"Why all the gloom?" He looked around, smiling at Phoebe. "With this splendid company you should be in good spirits!"

"Phoebe almost made me have an accident!" Robbie spat out.

Phoebe gasped. The arrogant, hateful one was back!

"We were exercising, and Phoebe had her head down a bit too long. There was no danger," Mam said.

Esmond nodded. He leaned over to pluck the coil of rope from the water. He was clearly puzzled, so Mam quickly explained how it was being used.

"Ingenious," he said admiringly.

"Uncle Esmond, we're finished with lessons. May I go riding on Hawk with you?" Robbie asked pleadingly.

"That animal is too spirited and frisky, Robbie. Someday you'll have a nice pony all your own to ride. And I imagine," he turned a warm smile to Phoebe, "that there's someone else who would like a pony to ride. Am I right, Phoebe?"

"Oh yes! That would be ever so nice!" Her eyes were shining at such an exciting thought.

"Mrs. Ogilvie, I'll take this young fellow with me to feed Hawk a sugar, then deliver him back to the manor before I ride."

Mam and Phoebe watched them walk away. It was clear from the way Robbie clung to his uncle's hand that he was once again the helpless victim. With one difference; he now knew they would not betray him.

Mam shook her head sorrowfully. "Poor Robbie," she said. "Poor, unhappy Robbie."

In the days that followed more than once Mam and Phoebe thought they were the ones deserving of sympathy; Robbie was even more assertive, arguing and disagreeable about every idea Mam put forth about lessons.

"He knows we aren't going to tell his secret, so he's letting us know he's in command," Mam sighed one evening. "It's understandable, but trying," she said.

On a day off she and Phoebe met Myrtle Stinchcomb in the village tearoom. They sat in a cheery, sunlit corner enjoying tea and sandwiches.

"Not as tasty as yours, Millie," Myrtle offered charitably.

"Those days seem a long time ago, Myrtle. But we're doing fine, Phoebe and I. My wages are fair, and we have free time, like this."

"Can the boy learn, Millie? I mean..is he _normal_?" At Mam's nod, she went on, "Good! The things I've heard! But seems more like he needs a good dose of the cane!"

All the way home Phoebe thought about something Myrtle Stinchcomb had said; Old Daniel was still working around the cottage as far as she knew. Phoebe hadn't thought about the peep place in the wall for a long time. If only she could be there all by herself!

The chance came unexpectedly the very next day. Mam announced that while she taught sums to Robbie, Phoebe was to take a sketch pad and draw the parts of a flower; dissect a bloom, draw the parts, and label, were the directions.

She lit out for the far reaches of the lawn where a bed of late summer roses still bloomed. Choosing one she separated it into petals, pistil, anther, sepal, and began sketching furiously. When finished she held out the drawing examining it critically. Satisfied, she put the pad on a stone bench, and hurried over to the hole in the garden wall.

With an eye to the opening, she looked through at the familiar objects; the swing, motionless and forlorn, Old Daniel's wheelbarrow with tools poking out of it, and a basket heaped with odds and ends of rags and paper. But no sight or sound of her friend.

Disappointed, she straightened, stepped back, and turned around to look into the amused eyes of Gavin Gardiner!

Chapter Twelve

Dinner with the Family

"Phoebe," he nodded agreeably.

She felt uncomfortable. Awkward. There was always Mam to help her feel unafraid around any of the family. Acceptable.

"This is our chance for a nice chat, eh?" He propped his cane against the bench, and leaning over to pick up the sketch pad, examined the drawings with interest. "I say," he looked at her curiously, "what's this?"

"It's a rose--the parts of a rose. I was to draw and label the parts. It isn't very good," she confessed. "I was in too much of a hurry."

"Mmm-m-m. Perhaps. But I do see some signs of artistic ability in your work. Art can be learned, you know. Lessons-all that sort of thing." He put the pad aside, and beckoning with a hand, invited her to sit beside him.

"This wasn't an art lesson," she smoothed her skirt carefully. "It's more-uh-you know- nature study."

She wished she knew how best to excuse herself and leave. Should she stand, curtsey, and say she must go? Or stand, say she must go, and curtsey? Earlier memories of how cold and detached Gavin Gardiner could be came to mind, making her feel all the more nervous and uncertain.

It was with people like Old Daniel and even Myrtle Stinchcomb that she felt a warm approval of herself as a person. Well, yes, there were others, too..the staff people, and Esmond Gardiner, and Robbie's mother.

"You were looking through the wall, there?" he motioned toward the peep hole. "See anything?"

She shook her head apprehensively . She supposed he would think the same thing about it that Robbie did; she was a spy, a busybody. Or some other kind of snooping meddler.

"I was trying to see my friend," she said defensively.

"And who would that be?"

"Old Daniel. He still works over there. Keeps the weeds and bugs out of our vegetables. Well..not <u>ours</u> anymore," she finished lamely.

"Yes. I know Daniel Bacon, myself. He's done work for me many years. Fine man. Does good work." He stole a sideways look at her. "You-uh-miss him, I wager."

She met his gaze. "Yes. He talked to me lots. Old-er- Mr. Bacon taught me lots of things."

He nodded. "Good. It's good to have friends."

"Yes," she agreed, sitting back a bit farther and feeling more at ease.

"So, Phoebe, even though you miss your friend, Mr. Bacon, you <u>do</u> like living at Gardiner Hall?"

"Yes," she admitted honestly.

"And you and my grandson are friends, too." he concluded, smiling.

She raised her eyes to his in an unresponsive stare.

"You're not friends," he said slowly.

"He kicked me," she said. "Twice."

"<u>Kicked</u> you? <u>When</u>?" He was aghast.

"When we were saying the Blesseds," she answered.

"The Blesseds?" He was puzzled.

"Blessed are the meek, blessed are the poor, blessed are---" she launched out energetically.

"Ah yes, the Beatitudes," he murmured enlightened.

"And do you want to know exactly <u>when</u> he kicked me?" she was indignant.

"Well, I--" he began uncertainly.

"<u>Exactly</u> when I was saying, blessed are ye when they <u>despitefully abuse</u> you!" she recited dramatically.

"I see. I-I can understand that would be doubly insulting." He strove mightily for composure.

Phoebe looked at him closely, satisfied with his serious expression. Actually she felt much better, in the mood to take the conversation along further. Perhaps Mam's words would fit in here nicely.

"I think, <u>actually</u>, Robbie is a poor boy--" she began expansively.

Poor boy! Gavin Gardiner, clearly taken back, looked about the vast grounds and toward the grand manor house.

Phoebe sensed things weren't going quite right. "Uh--he's an unhappy boy," she said, knowing full well that wasn't going to wash either.

"<u>Unhappy!</u>"

Hastily she decided to go with some of Old Daniel's ideas about people in general. She launched out on a fast-paced exposition that left her quite breathless.

When she finished Gavin Gardiner studied her speculatively. "I gather, then, that you think my grandson is a--a"

They said it together, "Better-than."

Phoebe nodded gravely.

It suddenly seemed the best moment to take her leave, which she did, forthwith, after grabbing the sketch pad and murmuring something about getting back to lessons. Stopping after a few steps, she turned back to drop a hurried curtsey, red-faced at her forgetfulness.

Phoebe decided to say nothing about this meeting. What was there to tell? She hadn't given away Robbie's secret, and what she had told wouldn't get him into trouble. His grandfather wasn't about to cane him! As sure, so the old saying goes, as God is in Gloucestershire!

That evening as staff came together for supper, Decker came into the kitchen as they were all taking their places. He wore such a peculiar expression that one by one they stopped talking and waited.

"The master sends word for Mrs. Ogilvie and Phoebe to dine with the family. Starting this evening."

All eyes left Decker's face and settled on Mam and Phoebe.

"My land!" murmured Wicker. Other voices hummed excitedly. Mam and Phoebe sat still, not moving, until they were roused by all the good-natured encouragements and smiles.

"Well," Mam sighed, "we must go change." She looked about the group. "We will miss these good suppers with genial company."

"Here, here," their voices chorused.

Phoebe felt sad for she had found comfort in the big kitchen amid the chatter and merriment. In fact, though she took her meals in her own rooms alone, even Mrs. Lumley, the housekeeper, had become less formidable. She had, much to Wicker's amazement, instructed special cake treats be sent to the schoolroom.

Later at the long dining table, splendid with china and sparkling crystal, Phoebe sat across from Robbie. She knew their well-wishers would cluster excitedly around Monique as she went in and out of the kitchen to hear how it was around the family table.

Phoebe ate slowly, once raising her eyes to meet Robbie's stony stare. She knew he was not pleased that she was a mealtime equal. If she didn't disapprove of him so much she could almost feel sorry for him, having to keep up the deception and be very careful with every move he made.

Mam had looked at Phoebe questioningly as Gavin Gardiner welcomed them before dinner.

"Ah, here's our young philosopher," he said with a faint smile. He and Alice Lambert had led the way into the dining room, followed by Mam and Phoebe, and Esmond who saw that Robbie was seated in his place. There was little conversation until the after dinner coffee was served. Then Gavin Gardiner turned pleasantly to Mam.

"Mrs. Ogilvie, I believe your husband was a Cambridge man?" he inquired politely.

"Yes."

"As is Esmond here. It's quite possible they may have been acquainted." He sent a glance at Esmond, and a look of consternation moved across his face as if he were annoyed at his own forgetfulness of his son's loss of memory.

"What was your husband's work, Mrs. Ogilvie?"

"My husband was a tutor, sir. In Paris, and sometime later in London and Bristol."

"Paris, eh? And that's where you learned the language?

Mam nodded. "And my husband taught me, also."

"I lived in Paris," Esmond spoke.

Everyone turned to look in his direction. Alice Lambert dropped her eyes in embarrassment for him. Gavin Gardiner's cup was halted in midair, his face, a cold mask of displeasure.

"Yes, Esmond, that was when," he began patiently, "we were there for Robbie's appointments. We were at the clinic, you remember, and the hotel." He was about to change the subject when Esmond interrupted forcefully.

"<u>NO</u>! It was another time!" He was clearly agitated. Putting his napkin down, he pushed back, stood, pressing his hands to his temples.

"I must think. Please excuse me. I must---" and he rushed out of the room, past Decker who stepped deftly out of his way.

Chapter Thirteen

"Someone's Made Off with the Bentley!"

Later that evening when a knock sounded quietly on the sitting room door, Mam opened it to Alice Lambert who stood looking at her uncertainly from the hall.

"I wanted to explain about the awkward situation during dinner," she said, sinking wearily in the chair Mam offered. "I don't know how much you know about-" she began.

Mam raised a hand in gentle protest. "Please, Mrs. Lambert. Please don't feel it necessary to explain anything."

"But I do. I don't want my brother thought deranged or even peculiar. He's a fine man who has lost his memory, and has struggled painfully to recover it. Many times, like this evening, something <u>almost</u> comes back from the shadows. Did you know," she asked abruptly, "that he was married?"

"That's what I understood from--from a friend," Mam admitted carefully.

"You mustn't be embarrassed about knowing things concerning this family, Mrs. Ogilvie," Alice Lambert said steadily. "For the last seven years all sorts of tales have been carried about, some true, others absolute falsehoods."

"The truth is that Esmond met and fell in love with a girl in London sometime after he left Cambridge. She was a shop girl. Father was livid. You see, he had his own plans for Esmond; marry well, be a credit 'to his class' was how he expressed it. So, Esmond was disinherited." She gave a deep sigh, and walked to the window.

Looking out into the darkness, she went on. "I can't forget how heartbroken our mother was when Father wouldn't allow Esmond to bring his wife here even one time. He forbade any contact with them. Mother disobeyed him at least once. And when he learned of her having seen Esmond and met his wife---well, you can imagine the strain we all lived under for a long time."

Returning to the chair she continued. "One day a message came from one of Edmond's Cambridge professors. He was in Bristol for a meeting, and received a mysterious summons to the hospital... to identify an amnesia patient. It was a young man who had a critical head injury from a street collision. It was Esmond. When he regained consciousness he had remembered absolutely nothing...name, family, marriage..nothing!

"When he was strong enough Father brought him home. And so far, with exceptions of small snatches now and then, like this evening, he knows nothing of what happened in his life before the accident. And of course, there's no way of knowing that he is actually recalling anything when this sort of thing happens," she confessed, discouraged.

"Your father seemed displeased when your brother spoke about having lived in Paris," Mam said.

Alice Lambert looked at Mam with a wry smile. "But of course, Mrs. Ogilvie. Don't you see? Though Father says he wants Esmond to regain his memory, if he does..or when he does, he will remember her!

"But one thing I am positive of—Esmond's wife would have to be a most unusual, unselfish lady!" Alice Lambert spoke with conviction.

"And why so, Mrs. Lambert?" Mam asked politely.

"How else could Professor Hookway have been notified? Only by someone who knew Esmond and his connection with Cambridge! That would have to be Esmond's wife. From the looks of the clothing Esmond wore home, they would be unable to afford the best treatment.

And so, wanting him to have the chance for recovery, she gave him up," Alice Lambert finished firmly.

"Perhaps," Mam suggested, "she didn't want to be bothered with his care."

"No." Esmond's sister shook her head. "I will never believe that! My brother, Mrs. Ogilvie, did exactly what Father wanted him to do in the first place. When Esmond married that young woman, he, indeed, married <u>well</u>!"

Mam accompanied her to the door while Phoebe sat very still thinking about what she had heard. Not much she didn't already know. Except-the questions about Esmond Gardiner's wife. <u>Was</u> she the one who called the professor to the hospital? And if so, <u>why</u> did she do it? Did she really want Gavin Gardiner to find his son so he could get the care he needed? Or was she unwilling to take care of someone who couldn't even remember who she was? Phoebe considered these questions in the days that followed. Would there ever be an answer, she wondered.

The golden leaves and grain stubble were signaling autumn's arrival. Villages scattered through the Cotswolds lay serene, splashed with the placid beauty of autumn colors along lanes and hedgerows.

There was just something about the tranquil loveliness of the September and October days that lulled Phoebe into feeling more and more at home in Gardiner Hall. Not that it was any easier to get along with Robbie. He was still carrying out the charade with no hint of revealing that he had regained his sight.

One thing that made Phoebe happy was what she saw one morning as she looked down from a dormer window; below, mulching rose bushes was Old Daniel! She coaxed an excuse from Mam and could hardly wait to get downstairs! Rounding a corner in the hall she almost ran into Gavin Gardiner.

"I just saw my friend, Old Daniel! Mam gave permission to say hello!" She whirled away breathless, then turned back to gasp, "And good morning to you, sir!"

He watched her skirt disappear through the door. Recovering, he put his hand to his chin, realizing with some embarrassment that he was smiling. Thoughtfully, he conceded there <u>did</u> seem more to smile about these days.

"My, lass! You're growing!" Old Daniel looked her up and down approvingly. He was glad to see her she could tell! "And would ye be learning how to be a fine lady?" he asked mischievously.

Phoebe nodded seriously. "Much more than," she looked about lowering her voice, "Robbie Lambert is learning how to be a proper gentleman!"

"Oh, ho, ho, ho, ho!" He laughed so heartily his face reddened and his eyes watered. Mopping them with his big handkerchief he turned back to work still chuckling.

Before she left him Phoebe learned some exciting news. Old Daniel was to work at the manor from now on. And most wonderful, too, he and his missus were to move into the cottage! Phoebe headed back to the schoolroom humming happily.

She came upon Gavin Gardiner standing in almost the same spot of their near collision. She halted, regarding him steadily. Without warning she threw her arms about his waist, hugged him, then flew away leaving behind an old man speechless, but strangely moved.

November's chilly winds and cold rainstorms arrived. Classes were in the schoolroom altogether now. Dinner in the evenings continued formal, but pleasant enough, with no further unsettling episodes. Esmond Gardiner was politely detached, and Robbie had stopped staring across the table at her. She knew it took all his concentration to successfully play his game of deception.

Many afternoons Phoebe ducked into the kitchen to visit during staff mealtime. When they teased her good-naturedly about being gentry now, she took it with good humor, chattering in French--to Monique's delight--and parading grandly about the room.

Robbie was making up for lost time in his studies. He was good in sums, liked geography, and had an immense interest in Empire history.

"I do believe someday you'll be in Parliament, Robbie," Mam remarked as they closed their books one November morning. He laughed at that, but Phoebe knew he liked Mam's compliments.

As Mam prepared worksheets, Phoebe finished up a watercolor. Robbie wandered over to the window and looked out at the cold misty landscape.

"There goes Uncle Esmond for a ride on Hawk," Robbie said. Phoebe and Mam went to look at Robbie's uncle striding toward the stable in his breeches and fleece jacket. The three watched until he disappeared through the trees.

"Too cold to ride today. And too wet. When I have my pony, I'll not make him go out on a bad day like this one!" Robbie declared.

"It doesn't seem cold to a horse," Phoebe answered. She felt loyal to Esmond Gardiner and resented Robbie's critical remark.

Back at lessons again, they settled down to French grammar and a discussion about the Loire Valley and its vineyards. Lunchtime came and Mam led the way downstairs to the dining room. Phoebe fancied one of Wicker's steaming hot stews on a dark, dismal day like this, while Robbie hoped for something with fluffy dumplings.

They sat a long time waiting. Slowly they began to sense an ominous stillness, a feeling of being quite alone and forgotten. When Della finally entered with salads and fruit plates, she was red-eyed and sniffling. At about the same time, Decker and Mrs. Lumley walked through with solemn drawn faces.

Mam put her napkin on the table and stood up. "I shall find out what is wrong," she said, determined.

Alice Lambert came into the room pale and trembling. She looked at Mam and Phoebe, reading the unasked question in their eyes.

"It's Esmond," Alice Lambert's voice quavered. "Hawk came back to the stable with no rider. Hardow and the men have been out, but cannot find him. He may be lying somewhere in this misty muck hurt--cold, injured!"

Mam drew her breath in sharply. Phoebe and Robbie sat quite still.

"Alice!" Gavin Gardiner's voice came from the doorway. "We've just discovered the car is gone! Someone's made off with the Bentley!"

Chapter Fourteen

Esmond's Disappearance

As night fell the manor was ablaze with lights, throbbing with confusion. The search was now two-fold; for Esmond and the car. The constable's squad had found the place where it seemed likely Hawk and Esmond had parted ways--a path wending through a tree-lined lane, rocky and steep. He showed a bit of cloth found hanging from a low branch to Alice Lambert. She identified it at once.

"He has a scarf of this, and often wears it when he rides," she said, fingering the material.

The constable nodded, satisfied. "It appears he may have ridden down that path, maybe the animal stumbled, and the young man took a tumble. There are ground markings that could have been made by someone taking a fall," he surmised.

"But a bit farther on, there are fresh footprints. Your people say they didn't search in that area," he looked at Gavin Gardiner.

"I'm thinking, while it doesn't make sense exactly," he cleared his throat, "that your son took that fall. He may have taken a hard thwack on the head, maybe lay stunned quite a time. But then sir, I have to believe he came back to the manor, and somehow without being seen, drove that car away. Now, we don't know why he would do that, do we?" He continued looking at Gavin Gardiner, getting no help from his stony expression.

"You see, sir, in the garage, there are heel prints with bits of leaf-encrusted dirt right where a driver would get into the car. Your man Trevor," he hurriedly consulted a paper he was holding, "yes,

Trevor..is certain those prints weren't there after he washed down the floor this morning."

Still no response. Gavin Gardiner stared at the ceiling, finally shaking his head in rejection of the idea. Several of the constable's men standing around looked away, feeling uncomfortable and in the way. They shifted from one foot to the other eyeing the old gentleman sympathetically.

Alice Lambert led Robbie away to his bedroom, and Mam went upstairs to tuck Phoebe in the big four-poster bed. It had been an exhausting day, and not over yet. A pall of despair had settled over the entire household.

"Where could he be, Mam?" Phoebe pulled on her flannel gown and climbed into the big bed. She felt wide-awake, too troubled to ever go to sleep.

Mam sat on the side of the bed, pulling Phoebe close. They sat without talking, thinking about the man who had disappeared. He had been very kind to them both since they arrived at Gardiner Hall, and Phoebe didn't like to think of him out there in the dark, maybe driving around, not really knowing where he was going or <u>why</u> he was going.

Mam squeezed Phoebe, settled her back on the pillow, and after pulling the covers up to her chin, placed a soft kiss on her cheek.

"Try to sleep, dear. Our worrying will be no help. I'm going back downstairs to see if Mrs. Lambert and her father will eat something. They ate so little at dinner I'm sure they need a tray. I'll be back shortly."

Phoebe lay staring at the ceiling. She tried to keep her eyes closed, but sleep would not come. Finally she made up her mind to slip out of bed and see if she could hear anything from the head of the stairs. She sat there, peering down through the balusters as the constable and his men were leaving.

"We'll be back early tomorrow morning, sir, and should there be news through the night, we'll be here immediately. With the description of the car and its registration, we should have that picked up shortly." The group of men, murmuring their good wishes, went off into the night, and Decker closed the door quietly behind them.

"I'm a bit hungry, Alice," Gavin Gardner said weakly.

"Yes, Father, I know. Mrs. Ogilvie is getting a tray from the kitchen for us. Let's go into the library to wait."

Their voices, continuing from the open door, were so much lower that Phoebe moved farther down the stairs until she could plainly hear.

"I suppose you've realized another possibility in all this, Alice."

"Yes. Of course I have."

"Can it be possible, do you think?"

"It's been a possibility for seven years."

"And I've yearned for it and feared it for that long," he said.

"Alice, am I to lose him, again?"

"You haven't really had Esmond these last years, Father," she said, gently. "He's not a whole man, just a restless shadow waiting.. waiting for sunlight to drive the shadows away. He's a tortured man, you have to know that."

"All I've ever wanted for Esmond is what's best for him, Alice," he said defensively.

"You've wanted what _you_ thought was best for him. Unfortunately for Esmond, your ideas and his were far, far apart."

"You've always thought I should have tried to find her!" he accused.

"Yes."

"How _could_ I?" he demanded. "The hospital said she disappeared. Just didn't come back. No address, nothing. How could I locate a ghost?"

"What may turn out to be more important, is how Esmond will think you should have tried to locate a ghost! For all you know, since you didn't even <u>try</u>, it might have been easy."

Phoebe didn't have to strain to hear. The voices were raised, quite distinct. When Mam appeared with a tray of sandwiches and tea, she saw the white-clad huddled figure immediately and pursed her lips with disapproval.

"Back to bed, young miss," she scolded softly. "Go now. I'll be up soon." She stood waiting as Phoebe rose and padded back to the landing and out of sight.

Back under the warm blankets Phoebe snuggled down, suddenly drowsy. She slipped away into a restless slumber, but didn't rouse when Mam came to bed sometime later.

Mam was already up and gone when Phoebe awoke the next morning. She scrambled out of bed, splashed water in her eyes, looking glumly at her reflection in the mirror. Why did she feel so out of sorts? Then she remembered. She was anxious to hear if news had come in the night.

She dressed hurriedly. In the drawer where the handkerchiefs were kept was the box. The box with her locket. She looked at it lying against the soft velvet, the chain curled around so gracefully. Holding it up to her neck she admired the gleaming beauty of it, feeling cheered and comforted. Fastening it about her neck, she tucked it under her dress. She was sure Mam would not mind her wearing it.

Downstairs Mam, with all the family, helped themselves at the sideboard to breakfast. It was a solemn group, Monique giving only a slight smile Phoebe's way as she put hot breads on the sideboard.

"Good morning, Phoebe," Alice Lambert smiled at her. There were dark circles under her eyes. Robbie looked up without speaking.

Mrs. Ogilvie, there will be lessons as usual this morning," Gavin Gardiner's voice was weary.

Mam nodded. Phoebe was disappointed. She could tell there had been no news, and had hoped to be downstairs when the constable arrived.

But it was not to be. Later in the schoolroom Mam started them to work as if it were any other day. Mam had long since dealt with Robbie exactly as she did with Phoebe. "You'll do the same work Phoebe does, recited <u>and</u> written," she had told him firmly. He had not protested.

Today as they did map study Mam announced she would go down for a lunch tray. She returned with a loaded one, spread a cloth on the reading table. No, there had been no word from the authorities.

Later, as she went to the door with the tray of empty dishes, she turned back to give some instructions; they were to take sketching paper, sit facing each other, and each make a drawing of the other.

It became a terribly amusing activity. They sketched, giggled, erased, and looked at each other closely before beginning the cycle over.

Suddenly Robbie stopped, his pencil in midair, as his eyes fastened on something. "What's <u>that</u>?" he demanded, pointing.

"What?" Feeling at her neck Phoebe fingered the locket that had slipped from under her dress.

"<u>That</u>!"

She gasped as she felt the chain yanked from around her neck.

"It's <u>mine</u>! Give it back!" Phoebe stood up, reaching out.

Robbie backed off still holding the locket, staring at it. He began to run, with Phoebe on his heels, demanding he return it. They circled the room, and when he reached the door, Robbie was out into the hall to the stairs, laughing excitedly. Phoebe was close behind, yelling at him angrily.

From the second floor they hurtled downward to the first. Robbie jumped the last three steps, looked about frantically, pushed open the library door, disappearing inside.

He tried to close the door against Phoebe, but she was too close behind and too determined. Heaving her weight against the door she pushed him back and barreled into the room. They faced each other, both breathing hard from the chase, Robbie still laughing while Phoebe struggled not to cry.

"Give it to me," she demanded.

"No! I want to look at it some more!"

As they stood glaring at each other the measured beat of the huge floor clock punctuated the silence. They both heard the other noise, some kind of strangled exclamation, coming from behind them. Turning toward it, they gawked in wide-eyed shock.

Up from a chair by the window a figure slowly rose. Standing there looking at them was the last person in the world they wanted to see!

Chapter Fifteen

The Reunion

Phoebe and Robbie stood transfixed as Gavin Gardiner' s eyes fastened on Robbie in a most frightful stare.

Hurriedly the boy held up the locket, crying, "Grandfather! <u>Look</u>! It's the locket you and Mama have looked for everywhere! It's my Grandmother's locket!"

His grandfather, appearing almost hypnotized, tore his terrible gaze from the boy's face to the locket.

Phoebe was grabbing for it, protesting in tears. "It's <u>mine</u>! Give it to me!"

Gavin Gardiner took the locket, holding it out of her reach. He pressed it open and looked at the picture inside.

"Father, what is happening?" Alice Lambert and Mam came into the room, their faces clouded in alarm.

"It seems Robbie has regained his sight," her father said. "From what I have just witnessed he has been sighted for God knows how long!" He turned away to the window.

"Robbie!" Alice Lambert's glad cry rang out. Dropping to her knees she embraced the boy, weeping with joy. Robbie stood still, his head bowed. The room was so quiet. This was not the joyous, long-awaited occasion; Robbie had not told them about regaining his sight! She dropped her arms, looking at him, disbelieving.

"Robbie," she whispered, "you didn't <u>tell</u> us? You <u>know</u> how we have waited for it to happen! <u>We have suffered</u>..." her voice broke with emotion.

Robbie began to weep, his shoulders shaking. Instantly Mam was at his side, her hands pulling him close.

"And so has <u>he</u>, Alice." She didn't realize she used Mrs. Lambert's given name. "Robbie has been deeply affected by his father's accident. All these years he has believed he failed his father at that time. Sometime he will tell you how he has not been able to forgive himself, and you can help him be healed from that pain."

"But I beg of you--and you, sir,--" she spoke to the boy's grandfather who still stood at the window, "to please consider he is just a boy, and he needs your compassion..else he cannot be merciful to himself." Mam's voice was low, but firm, heavy with the stress of earnest supplication.

After a long silence Gavin Gardiner turned around. "Come here, Robbie."

The boy walked across the room slowly. His grandfather put his hands on the young shoulders, and looked down at the tear-stained face.

"You can see."

The boy nodded. "Yes."

"That is a matter of deep rejoicing for us all. We will talk together about the other important matter soon. Very soon. Alice," he beckoned, "come let your son know how happy you are at his recovery."

"Oh Robbie!" She flew to his side, hugging him close.

Then Gavin Gardiner turned his attention to Mam. Phoebe had a dread that he was about to ask how <u>she</u> knew Robbie could see, how <u>she</u> knew he suffered from a guilt, and why she didn't tell them about it all much earlier. But instead, he stood there holding out the locket.

"Mrs. Ogilvie, Phoebe says this belongs to her." The locket dangled from his fingers swinging back and forth before Mam's eyes.

"Yes. It was a special gift." Mam returned his gaze unwaveringly.

"That <u>cannot</u> be," he said flatly. "This locket," he opened it, holding forth the portrait of the baby inside, "is the one, <u>the very one</u>, I presented to my wife thirty years ago. After her death, I searched, Alice searched, the staff searched this house! We have looked <u>everywhere</u>, except it seems, in the place where <u>you</u> found it after coming to Gardiner Hall!"

"No." Mam said.

"<u>You found this locket in this house</u>!" He was becoming agitated. Robbie moved even closer to his mother while she looked from one to the other in speechless bewilderment.

"She did <u>not</u>, sir!" They were all startled by the voice from the doorway.

Decker stood there. "Mrs. Ogilvie did not find the locket in this house," he repeated.

"And just how the devil can you be so positive about that?" Gavin Gardiner demanded harshly. "What nonsense are you saying?"

Decker came further into the room, stopping in front of Gavin Gardiner who stared at him indignantly.

"Sir, you recall when Madam Lydia went to Bristol because her sister was ill. You recall that you sent me with Madam."

Gavin Gardiner nodded impatiently. "A ruse! That's what it was! I was nursing a cold myself, and couldn't go. She resorted to a lie to make that trip!"

"You forbade any contact with Esmond, Father," Alice Lambert reminded him in a low voice.

"You know, Decker, I found out the real reason she wanted to go to Bristol."

"So you did, sir. But Madam had a great longing to see her son and his wife. And their baby daughter. I was present, sir, when they came to take tea with Madam. And when she presented the locket to Master Esmond's wife for the daughter."

Like a thunderbolt the full meaning of what Decker said fell upon Alice Lambert and her father. They turned to Mam, stunned. It was Gavin Gardiner who managed to speak.

"You!"

Mam nodded, stiffening a moment against expected hostility. Then she relaxed, feeling only compassion for the two who were reeling under a great shock.

"I don't know what I expected when Phoebe and I came to Chestershire," she began gently. "Nothing, really, except perhaps to see Esmond now and then. I knew he had not regained his memory, else he would have come back to us."

She turned to Alice Lambert. "You were right, of course. When I went to the hospital, Esmond did not know me, or anything. The doctors said it could be years, perhaps never, before he recovered his memory. But there were doctors in other places, they said, who might be able to help him become whole again."

She spoke then to Gavin Gardiner. "There was no way I could provide the best treatment. Like a miracle Professor Hookway was in Bristol for a meeting. I sent a message to his hotel. I knew you would accept your son back without me."

Phoebe drew a shuddering breath. She was understanding everything being said, feeling dizzy from the jolt of it all. Robbie was staring at the floor, no longer the center of attention.

"Why do you call yourself by the name of Ogilvie?" Alice Lambert asked.

"My maiden name," Mam said simply.

"Did you and Esmond ever live in Paris?"

Mam smiled. "Yes. For a year. Then when were expecting Phoebe we came back. Esmond's mother came. Just after Phoebe's birth. Esmond was overjoyed that his mother held Phoebe. We had tea at her hotel. Esmond always kept in touch with his family through.." her eyes flitted over Decker who smiled slightly..." a friend."

Gavin Gardiner sank into a chair. This was too much. Too much. Finding out Robbie could see, that composed young woman over there who tutors his grandson is actually the daughter-in-law he shut out of the family years ago, and the girl-child looking at him so searchingly--his granddaughter!

He was feeling many things. Many things. But what was coming through most clearly of all...the searing realization that he had been responsible for deeply hurting people he loved, and he admitted to his own conscience now, people he most definitely could love if he did away with senseless barriers.

He faced Mam purposefully.

"Father," Alice said, uncertain about his intentions.

"Alice, please," he raised a hand, "if I haven't come away from all this repudiating my own folly," he shook his head wearily.

"Mrs...Mrs...." he groped, "I don't know what to call you. Is it Millicent? Yes, Millicent. I..I..have wronged you dreadfully. And my own son. And the beloved wife who meant the world to me. It is too late to make amends to her, but I pray it isn't to Esmond..but I hope you can..." His eyes, fastened to Mam's suddenly moved to look beyond her, and at the same moment a voice harsh with feeling, came from the doorway.

"Millicent!"

Esmond, disheveled, eyes reddened, with an angry welt slashed across his forehead, stood there. Her eyes met his, and as she gave a cry, he was across the room, enfolding her into his arms fiercely.

The constable spoke, "Well, sir, there's your young man. He was actually heading back this way when we came across him. Everything," he observed mildly, before touching his hat respectfully and vanishing, "seems all right now."

Esmond, his arms still wrapped around Mam, raised his head to look down at Phoebe. He smiled, reaching his hand out to her. She came to him smiling back.

"Phoebe, I'm your Dada. Do you understand that?" he asked softly. She nodded. There were things she needed explained, but this she understood!

"Well," he said relieved, "thank Heaven for that! There's so much I don't understand! I've lost time, so much time!" He touched Mam's hair wonderingly.

"You look the same, Millicent. The Same!" Then turning to look stricken at his daughter, "but oh, Phoebe, you aren't a baby any more! What I have missed!" Esmond clasped Phoebe close, tears glistening in his eyes.

There were other embraces, tearful words, and words of joy in Gardiner Hall that day. Robbie's recovery and his uncle's were proclaimed Heavenly Blessings when the family joined the staff for an evening Thanksgiving celebration.

By now the story was known. Lying on the ground after being unseated from Hawk by a low-hanging branch, Esmond slowly realized where he was and where he should be. He hobbled back to the manor, and unseen, drove away to Bristol. Back to his wife and daughter on Briar Street. His head throbbed miserably, but mile after mile, thoughts and memories, past and present, swirled as in a kaleidoscope until shattering Truth settled in clear fixed Reality!

There were things he did not understand, and questions that needed answers. But one thing he knew--that was his Millicent back at Gardiner Hall tutoring his nephew. And Dear Heaven, that was his Phoebe! His own little girl!

He recklessly reversed his direction, and was on the way back to the manor when pulled over by officers. He exuberantly explained he was going home, consenting to the constable's tactful offer to be accompanied.

Later, much later that night, tucked into bed by Mam and her Dada, Phoebe lay remembering the people and places who had been a part of her life: the cobbler and his wife back in East Bristol, Ambrose and Myrtle Stinchcomb, Old Daniel, the kind staff at Gardiner Hall, her new grandfather, Alice Lambert and her cousin Robbie. She wrinkled her nose a bit at <u>his</u> name.

But, considering it all, she felt happy and contented, satisfied that <u>this</u> day had truly been what her Dada called it a few minutes ago as he and Mam looked down at her lovingly.

"This has been," he said, exactly as he had at an earlier time, "a lovely day, Phoebe."

Epilogue

Villagers still gossip about the family at Gardiner Hall. But sooner or later they get the truth of it from Myrtle Stinchcomb who takes tea regularly with Esmond Gardiner's wife.

The housemaid, Audrey, went about feeding the appetite of the curious with accounts of her own early perceptions of the former Mrs. Ogilvie. "I knew she was more than tutor from the first sight of her!" she confided to shop clerks who nodded knowingly. The most exciting news she passed along concerned her returning to her old service as nursery maid when the new nursery was occupied in a few months!

There is a new tutor for Phoebe and young Robbie now--a bright young man who has both students composing French poetry--and is courting Monique with his own tender rhyme.

The old gentleman, Gavin Gardiner, is contented with his family gathered close. While he looks with great tenderness on his grandson, his heart has been captured by Phoebe's straight-forward approach to things, and he still chuckles about the "Blesseds" conversation! Phoebe's growing resemblance to her grandmother has not gone unnoticed. Furthermore, he delights in watching the two grandchildren ride their ponies across the meadows, their shouts and laughter livening his days.

Phoebe still perches on any available structure to chat with Old Daniel who continues to plant, spray, and weed the green growing things. He and his missus like living in the cottage, but he did repair the loose stone in the garden wall! Phoebe, busy with poetry, ponies, and plans for the coming baby, didn't mind a bit!

Alice Lambert has a serious suitor. She and the manor manager, Adam Mathers, suddenly noticed each other, and her father heartily approves of the match.

Young Robbie has mercifully found peace from his torment of guilt. His disposition has, to the relief of all, improved steadily. Only occasionally does he resort to the old habit of reckless threats. The last time he had a difference of opinion with Phoebe, he tried to bring her around with the same old words:

"I'll tell my grandfather, and he'll..."

But Phoebe, smiling serenely, interrupted, supplying an irrefutable pronouncement:

"<u>Do absolutely nothing</u>!"

After all, he was <u>her</u> grandfather, too!